Native Storiers: A Series of American Narratives

SERIES EDITORS: Gerald Vizenor & Diane Glancy

Mending Skins

Eric Gansworth

University of Nebraska
Press
Lincoln and London

Library of Congress
Cataloging-in-Publication Data

Gansworth, Eric L.
Mending skins / Eric Gansworth.
p. cm. — (Native storiers)
ISBN 0-8032-7118-2 (pbk. : alk.
paper)
1. Tuscarora Indians—Fiction.
2. Mothers and daughters—
Fiction. 3. Indian reservations—
Fiction. 4. Iroquoian Indians
—Fiction. 5. Indian women—
Fiction. I. Title. II. Series.
PS3557.A5196M46 2005
811'.54—dc22   2004014531

Set in Scala by
Keystone Typesetting, Inc.
Designed by A. Shahan.
Printed by
Edwards Brothers, Inc.

A patchwork dedication for O, who tore everything apart; for P, who helped put it all back together; for L. E. G., who showed me the way from the very beginning; and for the Bumblebee, still handing me the needle and thread twenty years later

Contents

Acknowledgments

As always, thank you first and foremost to Larry Plant, for speaking up and remaining silent, intuitively, at the most critical times. The long haul is what it is. A tremendous thank-you goes to Bill Haynes, who gave so freely without asking for anything in return. This novel could not have been written without these contributions.

Thank you to the following people, who read this book, in part or in whole, and offered valuable advice: Bob Baxter, Junot Diaz, Mary Pat Leahy, and Bob Morris. Thanks especially to Mark Hodin, who offered succinct and key insight into an earlier incarnation of this work that opened the door for a possibility I had not previously seen. A significant thank you to Keith Burich, who set in motion things I had never even imagined. I am additionally thankful to Canisius College for its support of my work, specifically President Reverend Vincent M. Cooke, S.J.; Vice President for Academic Affairs Herbert J. Nelson; Dean of Arts and Sciences Paula M. McNutt; English Department Chair Sandra P. Cookson; and the Joseph S. Lowery Estate for Funding Faculty Fellowship in Creative Writing.

Thank you also to Diane Glancy, for continued encouragement; to Gerald Vizenor, for enthusiastic support; and to Gary Dunham, who believed in my ideas for the unorthodox relationship between text and imagery used in this novel.

Nyah-wheh forever, to my family, for offering sparks to reignite the story, and particularly to my mother, for showing me the way back, after all these years.

While actual locations, legal agreements, and historic events are part of this work's backdrop, this is a work of fiction. Names, places, characters, and incidents either are products of my imagination or have been used fictitiously. Any resemblance to actual events or locales or persons, living or dead, is entirely coincidental.

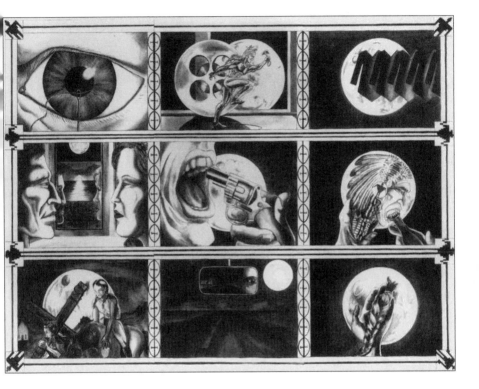

Prologue Opening Addresses

Partial Transcript: Keynote Address, Society for the Protection and Reclamation of Indian Images, Seventh Annual Conference, May 3, 1998

Tommy Jack Howkowski

Thank you. Welcome to the Seventh Annual Conference of the Society for the Protection and Reclamation of Indian Images. "SPRY," as we like to call it, is an organization dedicated to the eradication of clichéd and stereotypical images of Indians in whatever mass-market ways they have crept into the national psyche, by exposing these images for what they are, and by then providing positive alternatives. We have, in the recent past, successfully eliminated some of the most degrading sports mascots out there, but, until every last tomahawk has been "chopped," we will continue to be warriors for this cause.

In the year the organization was founded, 1992, the quincentenary of colonialism on Turtle Island, it was important that we consistently sent out the message to mainstream America that we were alive and thriving—that we were, indeed, spry, and now, seven years later, as that celebration fades from the public consciousness, our presence is even more significant.

My name is T. J. Howkowski, and I am this year's conference host. Some of you might recognize me from an appearance on the television show "Justice Scales" last season, in an episode concerning repatriation and adoptions, but only if you didn't blink. Or maybe some of you know me as Professor

3

Howkowski, in the theater department here at the college, and maybe even some of you know me as "Frederick Eagle Cry's son," or, as I am called back home on the reservation, at Tuscarora, where my good friend Dr. Anne Boans also hails from, "Fred Howkowski's boy." Given that bit of history, it is with tremendous pleasure and an overwhelming sense of honor that I introduce tonight's keynote presenter.

Dr. Anne Boans (Tuscarora) was born and raised in the city of Niagara Falls, New York. Her relations had always lived among their people within the borders of the Tuscarora Nation until the introduction of the hydroelectric water reservoir at midcentury, in which the government forced the Tuscarora Nation to sell nearly a third of its precious small amount of tribal land, homes bulldozed and whole families forever displaced under rock and earth and hundreds of thousands of gallons of water, ensuring that much of New York State would have a consistent electrical power source for generations to come. The state needed the reservoir as a backup for peak hours of electricity-generating needs and believed this place was the most appropriate. So, again, indigenous families were removed in the United States' insatiable thirst for power. Dr. Boans's family was among those displaced, living near the border of their ancestral land but not wholly of its national psyche.

Dr. Boans utilized and embraced the unique position this life experience has delivered her and, in true survivor spirit, has developed the keen eye of a cultural observer who is able to see the idiosyncrasies within a group identity and yet be distanced enough from it to offer sharp, pointed, accurate, and often hilarious commentary on the marginalized viewpoints of modern Native America. Armed with several degrees and an impressive presentation list, she has been widely published in many prestigious art history and culture journals, and her monograph on Indian humor in art has recently gone into its second printing. Please join me in welcoming Dr. Anne Boans.

Anne Boans, Ph.D.

Nyah-wheh, thank you, so much for inviting me to deliver the keynote for this year's conference. It is truly an honor, and I will do my best to live up to your expectations. My presentation tonight is called "Threads: The Hair-Ties That Bind." I have prepared a slide show, from my personal collection, of our visual national obsession with stereotypical images of Native America, particularly as manifested in images of braids, as somehow representing the pinnacle of Native identity.

My collection began years ago, when, as a teen, I struggled with the concept of my own identity, attempting to explore where I fit into larger communities, and, admittedly, my initial acquisitions were not made with any sense of cultural juxtaposition at all. I celebrated these images, trying to find my way home in them. In truth, a fair number of these slides did not originate in my own collection but, instead, were borrowed and photographed from the homes of relatives and friends, where the works are displayed with full admiration and embrace and not even the slightest trace of irony.

I have envied some pieces for their succinct capturing of deep cultural confusion and have offered to purchase these outright from the current owners, but in each case my advances have been rebuffed. The owners would no sooner give up these odd icons than they would family members. And, while he is not here, I always publicly thank my husband for aiding me in the procurement of items for my collection. He has the most amazing eye for finding outrageous items that dialogue with this outright exuberant embrace of stereotypes, but I have never dared ask him if he is buying them with culture critique in mind.

As an example, the item in this first slide was a gift from my husband for our seventh anniversary. Here we see a highly traditional bust of a Lakota in war bonnet, mouth wide open, presumably in full war cry, thick braids trailing out from beneath this explosion of feathers surrounding his face. Please note, this item is a bottle opener, the stainless steel lip that catches the bottle cap discreetly embedded behind the resin Lakota man's impressive row of front teeth. So, whenever the person who owns this opens a bottle of beer, the Lakota gets the first drink.

My husband purchased this item at one of the many tax-free cigarette shops that litter most contemporary reservations, where, presumably, a majority of the patrons are going to be peoples of indigenous origin. This in itself speaks volumes about niche marketing and our own communities' involvement in the perpetuation of these stereotypes. In all fairness to my husband the bottle opener was not the only anniversary gift he presented me that year. He also handed me a down payment receipt on a mobile home, which allowed us to move back among our people, where we continue to live, on land that has been his family's since the reservation's inception.

This next slide I have included especially for our esteemed host. I am sure you recognize these plastic Native warrior figures from when you were children, either playing with them or knowing other children who had them and envying them. These were produced in an era in which children's action fig-

6

ures did not come with articulated limbs, and, as a result of the immobility of the figures, they were generally produced in poses suggesting elements of their presumed social standing and class designations. In direct contrast to the other western-themed character figures—the cowboys—who were frequently produced standing surefooted and broad shouldered, hats cocked at jaunty angles as they gracefully slid their revolvers from hip holsters, the Natives were most commonly posed flailing about, limbs stretched far, defying the laws of anatomy and physics. Ever present on these figures, again, thick dual braids mimic the movements of said warrior, frozen in mid-sweep from the warrior's head, two angry vipers, arched and ready for attack.

In this detail from that group of figures we have the local connection I mentioned a few moments ago. While I have found no conclusive evidence that this identification occurred anywhere other than within the borders of our community, it has generally been agreed upon by those of us living here that this figure was based on none other than Fred Howkowski, a.k.a. Frederick Eagle Cry, a.k.a. T.J.'s father. Fred Howkowski had left our community in the 1960s to follow a dream of acting in the movies. I explored his career in depth in my dissertation chapter and subsequent paper, "Silent Screams: The Indian Actor as Angry Landscape in the American Film Western." It is paramount to note that our small local community so embraced these stereotypical images that it chose to identify one of these pieces of molded plastic with its own native son.

The two items in this next slide, while to some degree different, hold at the crux of their metaphors exactly the same idea. What we have here are two collector's plates from the

7

Alexander Mint Company, which seems to specialize in codifying and commodifying images some individual in marketing designates as somehow "truly American" images. From dead celebrities to cherubic flights among the clouds, this company suggests in the global span of their themes that America is in love with that which is unattainable and in some fashion legendary. Falling thoroughly in the pendulum swing between gorgeous foreign dead royalty and handsome yet brusque dead millionaire racecar drivers, we find more of this stereotypical fascination with a particular image of the indigenous peoples of this continent.

On the left we see an image we have seen just a few moments ago, at the beginning of this presentation—the ubiquitous war bonnet–wearing Lakota man standing among the equally ubiquitous buttes and mesas of the American West. And on the right, also in Lakota motif, a young woman, who we might suspect would be referred to as "maiden" in the advertising literature for this particular item, dressed heavily in a beaded buckskin outfit, kneeling subserviently in an overgrown meadow. The metalanguages of these two images, the relationships each figure has with its particular setting, are extremely sexually charged. The mesas surrounding the man are tall and narrow, shooting straight up into the pure sky, clearly strong phallic symbols suggesting the man's virility, while the meadow in which the young woman kneels is flooded with wildflowers, suggesting she is naturally among those wildflowers, open, receptive, and in full blossom herself, begging to be deflowered, as it were.

While these curious parallel elements are deeply disturbing in and of themselves, other, even more alarming suggestions are made by the rest of the compositions. Please observe, in each case, the Native figure seems to have some nearly super-natural relationship with an animal, as if we were all dark-skinned Dr. Dolittles, chatting up our animal friends. Signifi-cantly, though, in both cases the relationship is an ominous one, speaking of impending betrayal. The Lakota man holds out his arms, and a bald eagle lights gracefully on the man's wrist, and from what is the man's head accoutrement made primarily? Eagle feathers! Similarly, a spotted fawn rests its head on the young Lakota woman's lap, contentedly nibbling on some wildflower—that would be the young Lakota woman's lap . . . covered in deerskin!

In both cases these individuals are clearly gorgeous and toned, as if, when not cavorting with their animal friends, they are spending much time at Gold's Gym or, in this case, Red's Gym. Are these supernatural gym rats using their unearthly powers merely to cultivate new wardrobe accessories? Again, in both cases, regardless of all other visual dynamics, the one consistent element that tells us explicitly these must be Na-tives of the Americas—these thick shiny, nearly shellacked-appearing braids—stream from their heads dramatically.

The next slide offers a new twist on the braid motif. I found this in a gallery at the center of town in old Santa Fe, on the plaza, when I was delivering a paper at a conference sponsored by the Art Institute. That it was painted on black velvet, of course, truly set the tone for the piece, but I suspect it would have been as absurd had it been rendered in more traditional fine art techniques and materials.

The painter was selling the work himself, but I did not dare ask him for any further clarification. I feared any dialogue with the artist might ruin what was plainly evident in the piece. The artist called this piece . . . *Jesus and the End of the Calvary*

Trail. As we could have guessed from the title, the painter has merged the image of Christ and one of the stations of the Cross with that old western classic, *The End of the Trail*, where the downtrodden Native brave and his nearly broken horse head to the sunset of their lives, engaging these two characters as fellow travelers, a not unoriginal image in its own right, but note! Not only does the dying brave wear braids, but Christ himself has tied down his wavy locks in a herringbone braid as well! One can only speculate that the priest and nuns in the church far off in this painting's landscape must need hair ties as well. The style in which this piece was painted clearly harks back to an earlier era, rejecting the strides made by such contemporaries as Quincy Fisher or Janis SpringBee.

Shirley Mounter 2001

Yes, that's my daughter, shooting off her mouth in public again, though she calls herself Annie out here on the reservation, and she leaves all those other extra letters off, too. Ha! I could get up there and tell things better. I could tell the truth, but they don't usually want to pay so much for that. I was with her in Santa Fe when she bought that piece off that painter, and what she's not saying up there on the stage, with all those other fancy Indians in their coordinated beadwork and fashion ribbon shirts, pretending it's so quaint that someone got fry bread catered for their gathering, is that she saw that painting there, all right, but the rest of the story is a little different. She might say she fell in love with it right then and there, but she still negotiated down, because she said the people in the background weren't clear enough to show what they were. The painter said, "I know what they are," but that wasn't good enough for her, and she made him knock twenty-five off the final price.

But I wouldn't say anything even if they asked me up there on that stage with my daughter. She lets me keep my lies and half-truths, and I let her keep hers. She did until now, anyway. She's a smart one, and I always figured she'd just chosen not to ask me those questions, but I also knew they would come, had even practiced how I might answer them over the years, on occasions when I've been alone.

The answers in my pretend conversations haven't always been the same. Sometimes I said, "No, are you crazy?" Other times, "Yes, and I'm sorry I never told you before." Most often it was something in between, an "It's possible," which you'd think might be an easier answer, but it truly wasn't. It takes into account both possible paths Annie might be looking for and implicates me without giving her any satisfaction. I leaned more toward that one because it seemed to suit the reality of my life.

"Ma!" she said, firm, when I picked up the phone this morning. I was drinking my first morning cup and had worked my way through part of the newspaper. "You busy? I'm coming over in a while. How full is the back bedroom?" she said. Her mother-in-law's TV was on in the background with those overly perky eight in the morning people.

"Odds and ends, as usual, why?" I said.

"I have something I need to talk to you about, so don't leave, okay? See you in a bit." Where was I going to go? I didn't even own a car. I had to rely on my boy, Royal, or anyone else who stopped by to give me rides to the store or wherever, if they were going. I have to do my shopping by the needs of other people's bellies and hope we're hungry at the same time of the week. She hung up, and I went to clear the back bedroom of my things and see what I might do with Royal's stuff, too.

I knew, hanging up, that, when she got here, there was likely to be some major shift in her life, and I was going to be the one cleaning up again, putting things back together.

I had already guessed Annie's mother-in-law had more than a hand in this. Martha Boans has never been the easiest to get along with, and we go way back, Martha and me, but my Annie knows the good side of a fight, too. My daughter used to always like the city life, said it toughened her up, but that's not really true. She liked being anonymous, walking down the street, changing her curtains, buying a new car, and not having a couple hundred other people commenting on these things, which is the way it is out here. It took some getting used to, I'd be the first to admit, but I had a head start. I'd spent all my growing up years here and some of my adult life, before the state uprooted us like bad teeth. The nerves inside those teeth supposedly die when they're yanked, but, I can tell you, they throb for a long time, and then they only grow sleepy. Those nerves never die.

I'd known Martha for years, and our shared history was one of complications. So, when my daughter married her son, Dougie, it was just another level. Then, on their anniversary seven years ago, two things happened, and Annie felt the yank, deep, and I swear, she still to this day throbs with it and believes Dougie somehow set up both those things to bring her to this point. The first thing was his gift. The second, who could say why it happened? These stories fold, cross over, split, and reassemble themselves, and, though we'd known each other for years before, the first pulled thread was probably the one where my husband sold my house to Martha's husband on a drunk one night, and we didn't know a thing until after money and paper had exchanged hands.

Part One Feeling Bolts

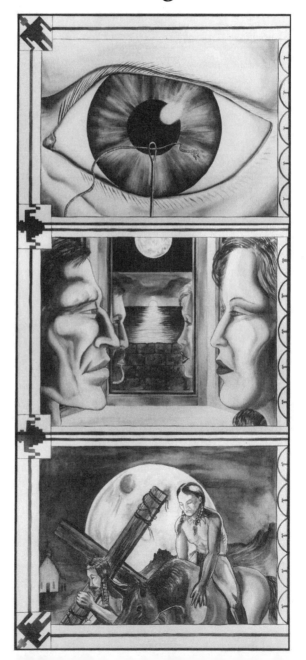

Chapter 1 Switching Foundations

Shirley Mounter 1957

"A thousand bucks," Harris said, spreading the bills out across the table. It was more money than I'd seen at one time in the entire three years we'd been married. "Count them, Baby, and count them clean." Ulysses S. Grant looked out at me twenty times, frowning as he does, hiding the sunflower-patterned oilcloth covering the card table in our kitchen.

"That's all they're giving us for the land?" I asked, looking out the window at the little sugar pear tree I planted when we moved here. It was taking root nice and might even bear in the coming year. Might have, anyway, if things had turned out the way they were supposed to.

"The land? Shit no, they ain't giving much of anything for the land. Nothing to speak of," he said, and then I knew that whatever the State Power Authority had given me in exchange for my land was gone, that my husband had signed my name to some piece of paper and had collected on it, while I fed and bathed our baby boy, Royal. Harris maintained that he was off "listening," down at the coffee shop below the hill, trying to get a sense of the real story on those mornings he was absent. Now I knew otherwise. He was striking secret deals. I had been attending the open meetings with the state, just like everyone else around here. The state told us they needed reservation land to build a water reservoir, to exploit the natural falls at Niagara for a hydroelectric plant. I didn't care if they wanted to turn one of the "seven wonders of the world" into a prostitute, but this was my life they were talking about. At first, in exchange for one-third of the reservation, they offered us a few different things, what amounted to nothing, figuring once again we were Indians and too dumb to know any better, anyway. For the most part they were right, too. We'd never had dealings with laws as they stood, but we did understand one thing. Money, everyone understood that. In the meetings they always talked vaguely, never giving us amounts. I imagine the chiefs knew amounts, got to see actual figures, but, if they did, they weren't talking either. Not to the likes of me, anyway.

Who was I to ask questions? A woman with hair as red as a flame, clearly a mixed blood somewhere along the line, though that exchange had happened generations ago, when no one was paying attention to that sort of thing. And here I was, married to an Algonquin from Canada, no less. No, I wasn't worthy of the chiefs' attention, so I had to get my information like some other people, picking out what I could in the way the chiefs and the state danced around in open meetings, keeping threads of conversation together, as they might appear, a piece one minute, another maybe not surfacing for another half-hour or so.

Sure, when the surveyors showed up in our front yard, with that ribbon, I just went out and kicked that one right in the nuts, and, man, did he fall like a tree. I wasn't alone. We were all out there, even folks who weren't losing anything. Most of the men were off working, still trying to keep some kind of income, but we were there, the women. Martha Boans stood right next to me, holding on to that little old baseball bat she used for clubbing Barry when he came home too ornery and drunk for her taste. The sore surveyor and the others left quickly that day, but, when they came back, they had police with them, and the police had guns. I decided to save the wear on my shoes.

The only two people who successfully kept the surveyors at bay with their land were Ezekiel Tunny, the chief who negotiated with the state in the first place, and Bertha Monterney, with her houseful of traditional dancers. What Bertha had on the state, or on Zeke, was anyone's guess, but it must have been some pretty big dirt. It was clear to everyone that neither her land nor Zeke's was up for negotiation. Their properties defined the northern and southern borders of where this reservoir was to be built, which left my little plot of land and the homes of a few others dead center for flooding, once the containment walls were built. Some, like Bug Jimison, just up and left, knowing before the rest of us that it was an impossible fight. He headed back home to the plot around his ma's house, but his wife wanted no part of that. She took their little boy, Hank, and headed off to the city.

Their marriage, I suspect, wouldn't be the only casualty of this way we lose things again and again. I figured at first that with whatever money we got we could maybe clear that smaller patch I owned in the woods, have a driveway dozed, get our house moved, and start over. I could plant another sugar pear tree, maybe even try to transplant this one, if my thumb was up to the talent required. But these fifty-dollar bills and the way Harris was answering and not answering told me this was the last money I was going to see for a long time, so I had better plan my moves carefully.

"How much?" I asked.

"Not much, I told you, Woman. You should be glad I got this. Always wanting more, that's just the way you are. No wonder you and that Martha are always together. Me and Barry have a good mind to head on back home for a bit," Harris said, sipping on his coffee, tracing the rings its hot bottom had seared into the oilcloth.

"You don't have a good mind for much, Harris Mounter. You go right ahead, but you aren't taking my car," I said.

"Your car? I bought that car."

"You might have gone to the dealer for it, but that was the last of the money I had saved before I left the factory," I said. Harris loved that car, said it was going to be a classic beauty no matter what. He said this style would stay around forever. I told him to look around town. There were hundreds of 1957 Chevys everywhere you looked. He thought that proved his point, and he took the money and signed us up for one, paying cash right at the desk, like a big shot.

"Well, why'd you quit that job in the first place?" Our conversations went this way. I was to blame for everything that went wrong in our house. He seemed to have forgotten that I hadn't gotten pregnant alone. Truthfully, Harris saw our little baby, Royal, as more of a nuisance than anything else, and I tried to keep him quiet or out of the way when Harris was home. This had grown more difficult with Royal starting to say a few words, but Harris was finding his way home less and less. I got Fred Howkowski to play with Royal, just so I could do some wash. Harris took credit for it, since he worked with Dick Howkowski, but I was the one who went over and asked Imogene if their older boy could help me out for some pocket change.

"Where'd this money come from, Harris?" I asked. "What did you give up in exchange, if it wasn't our land?"

"Woman, that is more money than you've ever seen at one time in your sorry life. Doesn't anything I can do make you happy? You have no idea of the haggling it took to get that much."

"What did you sell?" Beyond the sugar pear's meager branches, Barry Boans revved into my driveway in his own Chevy, the same as ours, right down to the color, but he might have owned his first. He pulled up right beside mine, and, when he got out, a metal tape measure rested in his hand. He saw me in the window and waved, smiling as he reached the glass.

"Just want to get some measurements so I can get to work on a foundation," he shouted, and walked to the far wall of my kitchen. Seconds later the tape measure stretched across my window, inches whooshing by as Barry walked through my flowerbeds to the far wall.

"You get out there and tell him we changed our minds," I said.

"About what? We ain't got enough to clear land and move this house, too. It was one or the other. I did the only sensible thing. You should thank me for getting this much. Everyone knows we don't have it. That we would just watch our house get bulldozed and flooded under like all these others. Boans is doing us a big favor, taking this shit heap off our hands."

"Get out," I said, and scooped up the fifties before Harris could lay claim to them again.

"You're gonna want to give those back now, you hear?" he said, as I slid them into my bra. I was going to need both hands. "I already got us a place in the city, but they would only hold it for a day until I could come up with first and last months' rent. I already gave them the deposit." He said these things quietly. "You're gonna like it. Maryann lives close by. She helped me find it." He circled around, the way he usually did when he was going for my hair. He always told everyone he loved my hair, when what he really loved was grabbing it and hanging onto me by it. I had been too vain all this time to get rid of it, loved the way it shimmered in the light, like embers and flame on a cold December night, but the costs were high. Sometimes after he'd gotten me by it, the roots ached for days, and I had to brush gently or lose nearly handfuls to the brush's teeth.

"I bet you know where Maryann Jimison's place in the city is. I knew there was more to their splitting than just losing their house." The only thing within reach was the cast-iron pan on the stove, but that would have to do. What I wouldn't give for Martha's ball bat at that moment, but she was busy, had already told me she wouldn't be by until the evening. I didn't know it was packing she was likely busy doing. She hadn't said.

"Bullshit," Harris said. "Though I hear the Bug lost more than his leg when he was hit by that car," he laughed. "You're gonna want to stop making me work so hard for this money. You know I'm gonna get it. You should just get our things packed here, because we're moving, Baby. You can come to the city with me, where I got us a nice place, or you can set your ass out on the road and take your chances, but, either way, we gotta be out of here in a week. Boans out there has the receipt you signed this morning."

The frying pan handle was still warm. I swung as hard as I could, whistling it past my own face. It hit flesh, slapping his meaty forearm with a crack, and bounced off. Thickening bacon grease hit the wall like a comet, shooting across the way. A trail slid down in long streaky rivers, staining the wallpaper I had picked out three years before. He wrenched the pan from my fingers and tossed it across the room. A second later he had my wrists and wrestled me to the table. His cup hit the floor and shattered, sending shards in all directions. Up to his old tricks, he gripped both my wrists in one hand, like he would at parties we had early in our marriage, exclaiming to everyone how small my wrists were. Even then, though, they could see him cinching tighter than he had to and the way he would only release me when I quit struggling.

He pushed his stubbled chin on me, and I could smell that he'd already been drinking that morning. I wondered who would even drink with him anymore, since he always got such a bad disposition after only a couple. Had to be his last drinking partner, who was at that moment measuring my house. He got one of my arms between us and pressed hard, one of his usual methods. While he moved my other arm closer, I hooked my ankle around the table leg and kicked it out from under us. We crashed to the floor, and I rolled away to the corner.

"Watch out, Shirley," a small voice near me said. Fred Howkowski stepped up, holding the tar bucket we kept in the corner for slops. He was only nine years old, and the bucket was almost as big as him. I hadn't emptied it yet for the morning, and he struggled with its weight. The stench of our waste came rolling out of it into the air. Harris never used it, said it made him wretch to even go near it. He always peed outside, off the front step, and where he went to shit was anyone's guess—likely a bar or maybe Maryann Jimison's place. I always thought this was just an excuse to never empty the pot.

"You wanna put that down, Boy," Harris said. Fred grabbed the bucket's bottom lip in one hand and the metal handle in the other, the same sort of movement he'd seen me use for years. I could empty a slop pail in one quick move and be back in the house pouring Lysol into it in two minutes flat and not spill one drop.

I heard the gurgling, even before it hit. The thick rain of waste hit Harris square in the chest, splashing and spreading as he struggled to climb from the broken table. A wad of toilet paper and a small pile of apple scruffs stuck to his shirt, as the dark liquid seeped into his clothing and glistened on the floor beneath him. He tore at his shirt. Buttons jumped like crickets as he yanked it off. His T-shirt beneath was just as bad, and he was going to have to pull that over his head. Staring down, he began to wretch, his mouth pulling down at its ends as if there were fishhooks embedded in his cheeks. The first wave of vomiting overtook him suddenly, kicking his body around with unseen force. He stumbled and slid face first into the muck and started another round of heaves. I grabbed the shirt he had just thrown off, while Fred gathered up the baby. We burst out the door and left everything else behind.

Barry Boans looked up, startled, and his tape measure came unhooked from my house, sliding back across my lawn like a snake. I wrestled the shit-covered shirt, until I found what I knew would be there, pulling the keys from the breast pocket and wiping my hands on the grass, leaving dark, foul streaks on the shiny blades. I had handled shit before. It wasn't so tough. We climbed into my Chevy before Harris made it through the door.

〈〈〈

I stood near Martha Boans, holding Royal in my arms a few days later, watching the group of men jack my house up from its foundation and get it onto a flatbed truck. Imogene and Fred Howkowski joined us as the men tore the chimney down, stacking salvageable bricks in the trunk of Barry's Chevy. Eventually, they got the house chained in place and slowly inched it down the road, watching the electrical lines as they crept along. I stood among the abandoned rocks that had been the foundation I'd helped to lay, myself, a few years before. Harris had stayed on the opposite side of the house the whole time. Eventually, people drifted back to their own miseries, bored with the uneventful way mine had played out. Harris wandered over, kicking dust and stones absently as he got close. He picked up one of my iris bulbs that had been uprooted. I didn't think that one would bloom again. It oozed some thick dark liquid as he held it out to me.

"What did you do to your hair?" he asked, reaching out to the place on my back where my braid used to lay. I stepped back, and Royal awoke in my sudden movement.

"What do you want, Harris?" I said.

"I want to talk to you. I got that place and moved our stuff into it. Fresh start, just you and me and the baby," he said, stepping between Fred and me. Martha snorted and leaned on my Chevy's hood. I knew what she would say, but I also didn't want my baby to grow up without a father.

"I'll get my things," I said. Martha and I made our way back to her shack. My house would soon expand her home by twice the space.

"You know," she said, "there's always a place for you on my couch, if you need." She paused and then smiled that bad smile. "After all, my house is your house, or something like that." We laughed and laughed, but, as we stepped into her yard, I got serious.

"And if Barry says anything? He might be your husband, but he was Harris's best friend first."

"If he says anything, I'll give you the bat myself."

"Nyah-wheh," I said.

"No thank-yous," she said. "I can't help what they've done, but there's no way you should thank me for moving into your house." I got back into my car, went back to the busted rocks that had been my foundation until a couple hours before, and picked up my husband to find out my new address.

Chapter 2 Parting Weighs

Shirley Mounter 1966

It wasn't long after we moved to the city that Harris was back to his old routines, taking my car, coming home only when he felt like it, and there I sat, in that apartment where the odors of cooking never entirely left, pregnant again. It seemed like it was happening every time I turned around. I swear, I would have another baby, and Harris would come and stay home every night only long enough to get me pregnant again, then he was off with his cousins and friends again or whoever. I had stopped asking long before then. Royal was getting big enough to help with the babies, not much, but he was company, he could talk a mile a minute, and Imogene's boy, Fred, who was eight years older than him, why, Royal just took to that boy like Fred was his older brother.

Fred added himself easily to my family. I don't know what went on at Imogene's house. He never volunteered information, but a lot of times Fred had bruises on him that didn't seem like the kind boys get roughhousing with one another, and he stayed with me anytime I let him. He was the double image of his mother, and I wondered if Dick Howkowski tried to leave some mark of himself on the boy, who carried over none of his father's features. I think, though, it was only half what was going on at his home that brought Fred to me. The other half of his desire came because my apartment was near the drive-in movies. Sometimes we'd spent evenings out there, parked in my Chevy, watching the goings-on playing out before us on that big outdoor screen as the characters' voices droned on those scratchy little speakers hooked to my driver's side window. On a good night we might even get some popcorn, but, even on "carload for one price" night, I could barely ever afford it. We discovered almost immediately after moving that the bay window in my apartment's dining room afforded a nearly full view of the screen.

Fred and I would sit in my bay window, visiting and watching the movies off in the distance, wondering what secrets those people said to each other on the screen, what secrets they kept from us. For my own part he was insurance, company when I was alone, and a way of keeping Harris in line on those nights he would decide to come home. As Fred got older, he became my babysitter, when Martha and I would go out, chasing our husbands down or even just sometimes accepting our lives and enjoying each other's company, instead. I never had to worry about Fred watching my kids and Harris potentially coming home and starting shit. Fred was untouchable.

Dick Howkowski was higher up in the ironworkers' union than Harris was, and he was a white guy, so Harris couldn't use any of what he called "blood pressure" to get his way. Dick might have married an Indian woman and might have lived on the reservation, but he held allegiances to no one but his wife and children, maybe not even them. Harris could talk almost any Indian man into the craziest things, somehow tapping into their shared history, making them blind to how bad his ideas were. That never happened with Dick, though, and Dick let him know it. This untouchable quality transferred over to his boy, Fred. Dick understood his position on the reservation, given to the whim of whoever was in power, so he stayed as neutral as he could, at least as far as those outside of his immediate family. As Fred grew older and reached the age of eighteen, that quality came in even more handy. Harris would try to indoctrinate anyone of legal age into his bad schemes but never Fred. If Harris were home when Fred came over, he either went into another room or left the apartment entirely.

"Shirley, I got to show you something," Fred said, coming in the door one day and sitting in the kitchen. Harris wasn't home, so he hadn't had to excuse himself. When Fred got his license, I had given him his own key to my place, but he almost always knocked. This time he hadn't, had even left the door open. I shut and locked it and sat down across from him at the table.

"Coffee?" He loved coffee, and I always had a pot on. I sat back down and looked at the letter sitting on my table. I knew what it was even without reading the contents. The United States Selective Service return address was plenty enough to tell me all I needed. That war overseas was getting more and more television coverage every night, and it was sure to be only a matter of time before I knew someone who might go over. Selfishly, I tried to project a date into the future where the war would be over before Royal reached the age of eighteen.

"You don't have to go. You know, you're a legal member of an Indian nation. Technically, they can't make you go," I said. We sat there a while as our shadows grew long in the afternoon sun.

"There's all kinds of veterans on the reservation. World War II, Korea, there's even some guys already over there now," he said.

"They made decisions," I said, and that was true. We were informed a long time ago that we didn't have to acknowledge the draft. The last generation believed they were part of America, but that was before the reservoir, the dike, when we were shown we really didn't matter at all. But he was right. There were boys from home who were already fighting, risking their lives. "You have one to make, too, I suppose. What day are you supposed to report?"

"I have to be in Monterey, California, Fort Ord, in less than a month, assuming I pass my induction physical."

"Have to? Sounds like you've already made that decision, then. One month, that's not a lot of time."

"No, it isn't."

"When did you get that letter?"

"A while ago."

"Your ma and dad know yet?" He shook his head. "Thought you were going to try to go to college."

"I was."

"There are colleges up in Canada. You have some folks over at Grand River, don't you? Don't your ma's cousins live up there?"

"Yeah," he said.

"Nice thing about living in a border town, you're just five minutes away." We sat there a while longer, and I eventually slid the window down, shutting out the city noise. It was May, but the sharp spring nights still had a taste of winter in them, even that late. "You wanna watch the movies? I think we got a new one tonight." Somewhere along the line, through those years Fred spent with me, we had started this game of making up dialogue with the movies unreeling blocks away outside my bay window. Sometimes they were just innocent, comical things, stupid things, really, but, as Fred got older, sometimes the stories he told revealed a different side of his life. I listened to him grow up through scenes of other people. He wanted to be the Incredible Shrinking Man, had hoped for the Invasion of the Body Snatchers. I liked watching Elizabeth Taylor tell Rock Hudson off in *Giant*, and we both always turned our backs when John Wayne's brutish mug came across the screen.

That night I learned a lot more than I had ever guessed. Fred had brought one of those Waterson girls over with him some nights before. Nadine was her name. I didn't know much about her, but I got a bad feeling when she was around. My fridge was always wide open to Fred for whatever he wanted, but he also respected that I was not the richest woman in the world. On those few evenings he brought her when I was out, that girl had taken liberties I had only extended to him.

"This might be your last chance. You don't want to die not knowing this feeling," he said, imitating a breathy, female voice, as some woman on the screen in the night sky held onto a man's suit-jacketed arm. The man looked distracted at first, hesitant, but then he slowly reached up and held the woman's bare shoulders. "I've done it, lots of times," he continued, "just not with you," now in a brusque, man's voice. "Then this is the perfect time," again in the woman's voice. If this had been on the television, I would have just shut it off then, because I think I had a pretty good idea about the rest of this story. It was one I'd heard lots of times before.

"She pregnant?" I asked, turning to look at him.

"Who?"

"That woman on the screen. The one trying to get that man to do something with her." He nodded and kept staring at the couple flickering out there in the night. "She got relatives in Canada, too?" Again, he nodded. "Is the baby the man's?" I asked finally.

"I gotta get going," he said, though neither character was leaving the scene. He walked back into the kitchen, picked the letter off the table, and folded it into his pocket.

"One month isn't a lot of time," I repeated.

"It's a bit. I'll see you lots of times before I leave. I hear I can also get weekend passes while I'm still stateside. I'll be back." He walked out the door, and I followed him to the back porch. He walked the two flights of outside stairs to his dad's car in the small parking lot behind my building, finally looking up, knowing I was still there, and waving as he climbed in and pulled out onto the street. Back inside, beyond the dining room window, the man and woman held one another. "I don't want you to go," I said in the darkened room. "The home you have isn't much of one. It wouldn't be so hard to go across the border." The couple parted slightly, ignoring me, and walked off screen through an already opened door.

I still had my Chevy. Harris had finally given up on bothering me for the keys and got himself a pickup truck to make his escapes from me easier. I got my drowsy kids up for a little while, piled them in the backseat with some blankets and pillows, and we headed to the reservoir. Why the state left a road on the reservation side is anyone's guess, but there it stood, and I threw the Chevy into second gear and drove the stone road up the reservoir's four-story wall. A few cars sat here and there. We weren't supposed to be on the dike, but the state wasn't very pushy in keeping us off of it. Sometimes they would come and shag people off but generally not. Mostly, it was a place for younger people. I was likely to be the oldest there that night.

That Waterson girl sat on a big pile of boulders thirty feet above the land that had been my front lawn. She was with a group of Bertha Monterney's dancers, and she seemed more than a little friendly with a couple of the young men around her. I wondered if Fred knew. I had seen this type before.

Certainly, she wasn't alone to blame. She hadn't gotten herself pregnant, and Fred must have been at least a reasonable candidate, to think the things he'd been thinking, but it appeared there were others in the running, too.

"Well, well," Harris said, coming up from behind me and wrapping his arms around my waist. I hadn't noticed him in the small groups of people I'd walked past, along the perimeter road, but he'd always had a talent for becoming invisible when he wanted to. Sometimes when Martha and I were out looking for our husbands, we would swear we'd gone through the whole bar and not find them. Then, as we would sit in my Chevy to see if they might show up before last call, somehow, at closing time, they would pile out of the bar with all the other drunks. "Shouldn't you be home with your kiddies? Or is your little friend watching them?" I pulled away, but he reached around tighter. "Now, now, easy. Remember, easy. You relax, and I'll let you go. We don't want to make a scene now, do we?"

"You're already making a scene, Harris. Let go of me, you pig."

"Pig?" he said, and laughed, making small squealing sounds. "You wanna know who's a gwees-gwees? Your little friend. He's not the innocent boy you think he is. Not two weeks ago I watched him going to town on top of that girl there, right on those very rocks, while the rest of us watched. He just dropped his drawers down around his ankles and climbed on up, drunk as a hooty-bird. We were cheering him on. He seemed to like an audience. Didn't take him long, either."

"You're lying," I said, though I knew he wasn't. Harris was not creative enough to come up with something as ugly as that. He knew what would touch me like a knife, but he could only recognize it and report. His cruelties were always borrowed. He could never invent those things.

31

"Someone else had to go and satisfy her after he passed out."

"It sure couldn't have been you." It was a jab but a weak one. He knew he had gotten me. I could feel his cheeks fill as he smiled into the back of my neck.

"You never had no room to complain." He paused and reached up to cup my breast, and I tried to move away again. His other arm easily gripped tighter. He leaned his mouth close to my ear and licked his lips. "He wears those little white underpants, like a kid. Not boxers," he whispered, giving the kind of detail I could, of course, never verify but that was too real to be anything but truth. "Guess he don't need the room to fit all comfortable," he added, then released me. "What are you doing here, anyway? I told you to never come looking for me. I'll come home when I'm good and ready."

"I didn't come looking for you. I'm not sure why I'm here. He stopped by tonight, told me some news." The thing I loved about Harris Mounter was the same thing I hated about him. Even without trying, somehow he got me to tell him everything going on inside me. He would use that information every time he wanted to hurt me, without fail, but he also used that information every time he wanted to make me happy. He didn't have that desire often, but all it would take was the right smile, the right touch, and I would be committed to him all over again, no matter how much I might list off in my head the terrible things he'd done over the years. I had said "for better and for worse," but that minister had never clarified the relative amounts of those experiences. Even if he had, all it would have taken was Harris's secret smile, the one I tried to believe he saved only for me, and I would have said yes all over again.

"What, that he's going over? Becoming target practice in those jungles we see on the TV? Crazy bastard. He should just up and go to Canada. I would," Harris said, rolling a cigarette with one hand and licking it slowly, with thought.

"How do you know he's been drafted? When did he talk to you?" I couldn't imagine, after I'd half-raised the boy, that Fred had told Harris first. I tried imagining that he had asked Harris for advice on how best to tell me, but there is no way on earth that conversation had ever occurred.

"He didn't. He told that little girl down there. That was one of the reasons she offered him a piece. Going-away present," he laughed.

"I don't think he knows that," I said.

"Of course, he don't. He's not so bright, that little friend of yours. So, where's the kids, anyway, if he ain't watching them?"

"In the car. Sleep."

"Any in the front?"

"Royal."

"I guess he can still fit on your lap. Give me the keys," he said, finishing a bottle of beer and whipping it out across the water. The wind whistled through its lip as it disappeared, splashing in the darkness.

"Where's your truck?"

"Boans took it, said he had promised Martha he'd be home tonight for some damned thing."

"Barry Boans kept a promise to someone?"

"Keys?"

"No, you can run your own drunk ass off the road, but you aren't risking my life or my kids' lives," I whispered. Harris could take the truth, but he couldn't take public embarrassment. It was one of his few weaknesses. "And if that means throwing you down these rocks and into the water, I'll do it or wind up there myself. Either way, you aren't getting the keys.

33

You can come home with us, but the first shit you try, you are out in the road." We'd grown used to living our lives without him, and I had seen enough people from home, young and old, die on the roads and had no intention of keeping their ghosts company.

"All right, let's go home," he said, and walked to the passenger door. He lifted Royal into his lap without rousing the boy. I took us down the side of the reservoir and crossed back off the reservation and into the city a few minutes later. I ignored him, choosing to look out the windshield and in my rearview mirror, but he watched me the whole time. He reached over to touch my hair, but I swatted his hand away.

"Now why'd you go and do a thing like that?" he slurred.

"You want to be with me, you're going to be sober. I'm not having you pass out on top of me again. That last time it took me almost a half-hour to get you off of me, and I almost smothered."

"Yeah, that was a good one," he laughed. "And when are you going to grow your hair back, anyway? You know, once you cut it in mourning, you're supposed to let it grow back, to show you accept the future."

"What would you know about such things?"

"I know more than you think. So, when are you growing it back?"

"As long as I'm married to you, I won't be."

"So, that's the way it is."

"That's the way it is."

"Hey, if I give you a secret, will you grow it back, even a little?" he said. I ignored him and watched the country roads become suburban roads and then city streets as we got close to the apartment.

34

"Okay, I'm gonna tell you, anyway, and you can decide whether it's worth a trade. That girl? She told him she's pregnant and that it's his. But it ain't his."

"How do you know?"

"I know things."

"Whose is it, then?"

"Don't know that, but it ain't his."

"Why would she claim he's the one if he's not? What would there be in that?"

"Of all the guys who it could be," he said, slowly, as if speaking to a child, "he's the only one with a foot in both camps." My husband always liked to act as if he was wiser than everyone around him and that he would only deliver his information when and if he decided his audience was worth it, but, really, all I ever had to do was wait. He could never resist.

"Indian and white. She wants to give the kid a fighting chance."

"How thoughtful." At the apartment Harris stumbled in ahead of us, leaving me to gather the kids. I woke them one by one. Royal was groggy but awake enough to carry one of the little ones, while I carried the other. We got up to the third-floor landing to discover Harris had let the outer door shut behind him, so I had to dig for my keys. As I got them, he opened the door from the inside, smiling.

"Guess what I found in the ditch?" he said, and laughed. This was reservation slang for an unexpected visitor. For years people would toss out unwanted animals on reservation roads, I suppose hoping the animal would be welcomed into a good home. Sometimes that worked out, but, as often, the animal found its way into a paper grocery bag, thrown up into the air in a field and used as moving target practice. A few bullets

35

were cheaper, for some, than trying to feed an animal when they could barely manage with their own kids.

I led the kids in to their bedroom, where they fell immediately back to sleep. Fred sat in my dining room, in the dark, looking out my bay window at the blank, dark screen those few blocks away. "Show's over," he said, as I walked up and stood next to him in the window. "Shirley, will you come with me to tell my folks?"

"When?" I asked, but he didn't respond. "Now? Well, I got the kids here and—"

"I'll be here. Going to bed," Harris said, removing his shirt and kicking his boots into the entryway corner. "Go on."

We rode in silence back to the reservation, and I watched the reverse progress of buildings. The apartment buildings gave way to narrow city houses, and then, gradually, the houses got farther apart in the suburbs, shrubs and trees growing more thick, then the wide expanses of lawn and garden in the country, and, finally, the bullet-ridden signs announcing the reservation and the dense growth of woods there, pushed back only sporadically with houses.

We stepped into the house, and I sat down at Imogene's oak veneer dinette she was so proud of, while Fred walked down the hall to his folks' bedroom. "Ma, Dad?" he asked, standing in the hall. I could only imagine what they thought, their son standing mostly in shadow in the doorway to their bedroom. While none of my children had grown to adulthood yet, the experience Imogene had at that moment was not one I would ever welcome. It could just not invite good news. Good news always waited for opportunity, but bad news came when it felt like it.

"What is it, Hon?" Imogene asked, startled. Before long we all sat at the dinette. I didn't know exactly what I was supposed to do, so I did one of the things I did best then. I put on some coffee and poured cups for the four of us. The younger Howkowski boy had gotten up, too, but Imogene had sent him back to bed. I suspected he stood in his doorway, trying to hear this middle-of-the-night meeting.

As at my table, Fred pulled the envelope from his jeans and laid it out in front of them. "Jesus," Dick said. Normally, I think this would have gotten him a slap on the arm from Imogene, but she just went pale and gripped the table. No one said anything or even moved for what seemed to be the longest time.

"Well, I can write my congressman," Dick said, finally, sipping from his coffee cup. "We'll see, maybe that'll do something. The union hall's supported him, now he can support us." He got up and dug around in their desk, I assume, to get that information, so he could call once the sun rose.

"I should get going," I said, standing. "If there's anything I can—"

"There's something else," Fred said. He looked out the front window, but the only thing there was a dense growth of trees and a path he had ridden his bicycle down through his childhood. No movies there to fill this silence. "I'm going to be a father."

Both Imogene and Dick looked at me then at my belly. I couldn't help it, I burst out laughing. "Not me!" It turned out to be the right thing. We all laughed. There was little else to do. It was either that or cry, and I suspect we were preparing to save all of our tears for later.

❨ ❨ ❨

"So, did you save the day?" Harris asked, as I crawled into bed hours later. He reached over and rubbed my back, which felt wonderful. Even when he was gone for months at a time, he remembered exactly which spots were magic, as soon as he returned. He rested his belly up against my back, as his hand slid up to meet my breast again, and I could feel his intention stirring.

"How could you just watch him doing that?" I asked. It was my way of acknowledging the damage he had done but also my way of letting him know I had some weapons myself.

"Oh, jeez, Babe," he said, rolling over onto his back and sighing. "He's a reservation kid with barely a high school diploma. You know where that poor bastard is going, straight to the front lines. He's gonna be infantry, period. He'll be lucky to still have both his nuts when he comes back. If he comes back. How could I not let him get a little tail before shipping out? And that girl don't care. He sure wasn't the only one."

"I didn't ask how you could let him do it. He's a grown-up now, I know that. I asked how you could watch." Harris rolled out of bed and slid the boxers back on that he'd taken off sometime while I was out. He picked his jeans up off the floor, sniffed them, decided they were still clean enough, and put them back on. He walked out the door a few minutes later, and I didn't see him or hear from him again until almost a month later, at Fred Howkowski's going-away party.

It was a small party, just a few people pretending to enjoy themselves. Fred kept trying to cheer everyone up, goofing on them, wearing an empty planter on top of his head like an army helmet, stuff like that, and they all smiled politely. Just about every one of them gave him a hug before they left, even the men. I could see, whenever he wasn't looking at someone, they were memorizing his features, like they believed they weren't going to see him ever again. I couldn't do that. I had to look elsewhere—flowers, tablecloth, food, friends, anything. I had to believe he would be back. As Fred was about to leave, Harris showed up and gave him some money, "just in case," whatever that meant. Harris shook his hand and grabbed his jaw and shook it a little. Fred smiled back and patted Harris's shoulder. "You be good to my best friend, or I'm going to have to come home and kick your ass," he said, and Harris looked at me and nodded to Fred.

"I swear you and my old lady got something going," he said.

"Better not be," that Waterson girl said, and, though she was smiling, she clearly saw me as some kink in her plans for Fred.

"Just remember, if you run out of ammo, you can always throw the slop pail on them. Works every time," Harris said, leaving. The Waterson girl, Imogene, and Dick, and I took Fred to the Induction Center. I drove them in my Chevy, even with the muffler going. We saw him off at the gate. He held onto that Waterson girl for a while and rubbed her belly. "You take care of the kiddo," he said to her. "Let me know soon as he's born. You be good!" he yelled to her belly.

"Freddie, we don't even know if it's gonna be a boy or a girl," she said, rolling her eyes and smacking him on the top of his head.

"He's a boy, I can feel it. See, feel here," he grabbed her hand and made it rub her distended navel. "That's gotta be a boy."

"Write as soon as you get an address, Son. I'll keep on the congressman and see what we can do. You know, if you were married, we could have put in for a hardship deferment," Dick said. That girl rolled her eyes out across the tarmac, studying the planes coming and going. "Anyway, I'll keep you posted. We've still got six months to get you out of this, right? A lot can happen in six months."

"Ma, I promise, I'll be careful, and I'll be back before you know it. Hey, no crying now. You know Indian women don't cry."

"Indian men, either." She wiped his cheek with a handkerchief.

"I'm only half-Indian, remember?" he said, trying to smile. "Hey, you sit by that phone tonight. If I fail the physical, I'll be calling you to pick me up. And, if I don't call, don't you sell that Chevy. I still want to buy it off you when I get back."

"You can have it when you get back. I promise, it'll be waiting for you," I said. We watched him walk into the building and then headed home. I dropped Dick and Imogene off and then that girl I left at Bertha Monterney's house, where people milled around outside.

That night I sat in the dark and watched the movies out my window, no music, no television, and waited until the last reel of the weekend triple feature played out and the parking lot lights came on, and waited until every last car pulled out of the lot, and waited until the parking lot lights went back out. Harris walked in some time later and joined me at the window, reaching around and pressing his soft belly into my back. "He didn't call," I said.

"Did you really think he would?" He took my hand. We walked to the bedroom and made love until we were both too exhausted to stay awake any longer.

Chapter 3 Connecting Flights

Shirley Mounter 1972

Fred's leaving for Vietnam was a gradual thing, after all, just as his eventual real leaving would be. After he shipped out to basic training, he would occasionally come home on weekend passes, and then even that stopped until his last weekend before heading over across the ocean. Not that I ever saw him too much in that period. He spent most of that time with the Waterson girl, which was no surprise, really. I did see him that Friday night before his big departure, but he was so jittery he left my apartment while the dancing and singing popcorn tub and ice cream cone bounced across the screen outside my window. He had always loved that part and had invented all kind of outrageous words to their songs, about seducing people to come and eat them. He would turn red with his vulgarity, though we had always laughed. There was no singing that night. "Gotta go, you take care of yourself," he said abruptly, and left me alone to watch the second feature silent.

A year later Martha and I and our old men were with Imogene and Dick when we first got the news about Fred. We were out bowling, of all things. To this day I can't imagine what brought us all together, other than Dick's team doing poorly. Harris and Barry were ringers, could bowl strikes with broken fingers, but were never reliable enough that anyone wanted them for regular teammates. If Dick's ironworker tournament team were doing poorly in the league, though, they were brought in as subs. The bowler with the worst average had to

41

pretend he was sick, and one or the other of our men would show up. The white teams knew what we were up to, but there were no rules about substitutions. The team was down, so the two worst had to be sick.

Harris had just gotten three strikes in a row and called to his opponents, as he did every time he performed this act. "My three strikes, and you're out!" he would shout, then laugh to himself and sit back down. He had me run to the bar for a couple of pitchers to celebrate, another part of his ritual. The tap ran out toward the end of the first pitcher, and I was about to carry the first to the lane while the tender changed the tap. As the second pitcher filled with foam, Gary Lou, Imogene and Dick's other boy, came running through the doors, nearly out of breath, and called my name.

"No kids, you know the rules," the bartender said.

"Just get rid of that head, I'm paying for beer, not suds," I said, and led Gary Lou out into the lobby. "What are you doing here? How did you even—" The Protestant minister stood in the glass entryway, waiting, not stepping one foot inside. I knew, suddenly, what was coming. I had tried to prepare as soon as Fred had left, but this moment was not the kind of thing you wanted to prepare for. To think about those things, practice for them, it's like you invite them, give an excuse for all those terrible possibilities to walk right on into your house and get comfortable.

"It's Fred," Gary Lou said, and the floor dropped out from under me. My head grew cold, and that feeling traveled down my body and into my arms. Everything was sharp and hazy by turns, in and out, like those flipping lenses they have you look through when you're being tested for glasses. That man in the white coat and the bad breath asking you, "Which is better, one or two? One? Two?" and you feeling stupid after a while because you couldn't tell anymore. How could these people continue to shoot billiards, drink beer, eat pizza, roll strikes, spares, the one-ten split? How could they continue to laugh? And that minister, why was he smiling? Gary Lou grabbed my arm and said something else as the pitcher fell to the tile floor and shattered and the world went dark around me.

The acrid odor of smelling salts got me back a minute or so later, and, assuring me Fred was fine, they pulled me along out to the parking lot and put me in the backseat of my own car. Lights flashed by in front of me as we merged onto the thruway. The world vibrated and rumbled as I continued to re-orient myself. Everyone else in the car shouted, animated, particularly Harris. He was still shouting, "My three strikes, and you're out," again and again, and everybody hooted as if hearing it for the first time. The lights whizzed past on the thruway as we made our way to Buffalo. Everyone around me continued to shout and yell, but I couldn't shake that initial sense I'd had about Fred. Harris pulled over and dropped us off at the airport entry then drove around to the lot. Dick Howkowski was the kind of man who could take care of any situation, no matter the pain, so I followed him, in case they were wrong in their belief that Fred had come home safely. I knew it was ridiculous, but I needed to see him before I would believe he was really back.

"You okay?" Imogene asked, holding onto my shoulders as we entered the revolving doors. "You sure gave us a scare back there. Gary Lou's still shaking," she smiled.

"Well, it's about damned time!" Fred Howkowski shouted, standing before us, big as life, a little rumpled, but in uniform. He picked up his mother and spun her around. In the year he'd been over in Vietnam he'd grown a mustache. It looked odd on him, a disguise mustache. "You guys forget me or what?" he laughed, as Dick shook his hand and clapped him on the shoulder.

"Welcome home, Son. They don't have any razors over there in Vietnam?"

"So, where's my car?" Fred said, turning to me and hugging me.

"Right outside, exactly where it was the last time I saw you," I said, holding tight. The ribbons on his chest pressed into me. I didn't know what they were for, but they clearly signaled he was no longer the boy who babysat my kids and talked to the movies out the bay window of my apartment.

"Hey, hands off my wife, Soldier," Harris said, walking in.

"I am nobody's soldier. Ever again," Fred said, sliding the cap from his head and picking up his duffel bag, which Dick reached for and took, immediately. "Careful, Dad. That bag's a little heavy."

"Ha! Nothing I can't handle," Dick said, shifting, a little off.

"So, uh, we'll see you all at the house a little later?" Fred said. It was only then that I noticed the Waterson girl, standing off to the side, holding that little one-year-old she claimed was Fred's. She'd said nothing the entire time we'd been there. "We've got some catching up to do first. Baby, lead the way," he said, heading to the revolving door. The old Fred would have been red with embarrassment, but, this new one, he knew what was on his mind, and he didn't care that we knew just as clearly.

"Okay, Son, we'll see you a little later," Dick said, lowering the duffel to the floor.

"Fred, is there anything special you'd like to eat?" Imogene asked as they neared the exit.

44

"Naw! We'll just get something. Don't wait up. Not sure what time I'll be back." Then he stopped and smiled, and I could see the Fred I used to know. "Really, don't go to any trouble, Ma. Just being home and in my own bed, that'll be good enough." We watched them walk out and into the lot, where Bertha Monterney's station wagon was parked, right near my Chevy.

Fred was in and out of all of our lives for the next two years, drifting about town in the car I had given him. Sometimes I knew where he was, sometimes not. Word gets around fast, and the Waterson girl disappeared as quickly as she'd come in. Fred had maybe not expected much to come of his time with her, and his expectations were met. If he had regrets about the way things went with that young woman, he never said to anyone. The little boy eventually went to live with Fred at Imogene's. Everyone had heard the story of how some Texas redneck had saved Fred's life and that Fred insisted the little boy have that god-awful name. I was more surprised not that Fred had such a bad idea but that the little boy's mother allowed it, to be truthful. She did, though, and that baby came into this world with the unlikely name of Tommy Jack Howkowski.

Those first couple weeks we drove around in my Chevy, doing very little, stopping to see friends, pausing at a bar when we felt the urge. The others around us changed nightly. Imogene sometimes kept our kids, sometimes Martha. The time Harris spent at home grew shorter than before. He was there the first couple nights, but he saw some change in Fred that made him want to stay away. One thing Harris always liked was the ability to scare. I suppose that was part of what attracted me to him, back when I was young and stupid.

I had likened that boldness and meanness of spirit to power. Harris was going somewhere, I was sure, but I hadn't seen that the only place he was going was straight back to his home reservation with that good-for-nothing friend of his. When we were first seeing each other, Harris could walk into the Circle Club, and people noticed. They cleared out of the way, gave up a place for us right at the bar, no matter how packed it might have been. He thought that was just the greatest, and at first I saw it through his eyes, saw respect. It was only later, when I heard others in the ladies' room stalls complaining about that Mounter pig grabbing at them. They asked each other how I couldn't help but see the way he was, and afterward I did see him through their eyes. It was as if they forced me to put on a pair of glasses I was unable to remove.

I saw him ordering our drinks, pressing himself into other women as he did, pretending it was so crowded these things could not be helped. I saw him hugging women we knew, a little too long and a little too low. Where I had always seen Harris as friendly and warm, I then saw he only treated women like this who were with men smaller than him. He was as interested in enraging these men as he was in getting whatever he received from these women. Sometimes, when we were home in bed and the kids were asleep, I could see the old Harris, the one I had chosen to marry, but he had usually vanished by morning, seeming for the most part to live elsewhere, leaving behind this other man and no forwarding address.

Still, I didn't give up hope and continued to chase him down some nights. By then it was mostly to get some money out of his hide so I could feed the kids and pay the bills, and in that way my husband was indirectly responsible for my meeting Tommy Jack McMorsey. To save money I had begun making my kids clothes, and, if I had enough left over, I'd make my own as well on occasion. I was wearing one of my first shirts the night I met Tommy Jack McMorsey in the Circle Club, one stool down from a freshly discharged Fred Howkowski.

"I like that shirt, Ma'am. Fits like it was made for you," he said, smiling. He was older than Fred but younger than me, maybe by a few years on each side. I recall Fred writing something about this guy having been in college before he'd been drafted, though the man in front of me didn't seem the college type.

"It was. Made it myself," I said. "Thank you for noticing, and for keeping my old babysitter alive, over there in the war." Fred blushed, not wanting his war buddy to know he had been the babysitting type before he got drafted. I smiled at Fred and held up my drink, letting him know all his secrets were safe with me, including the one about what he came home to, his boy living at Bertha Monterney's house because that Waterson girl was shacked with one of Bertha's dancers and holding onto the boy for support money. Bertha Monterney was a great woman, carrying on traditions and all, but sometimes turned a blind eye to questionable actions. Her one rule—she would take you in no matter of your circumstance, as long as you worked and you danced—left flexibility for other actions. Bertha eventually told the girl to move out or give the baby a better home, knowing the boy would wind up back with Fred, since he'd returned.

I don't know what it was about Tommy Jack McMorsey, maybe the way he smiled, the way he noticed the care I took to look my best, maybe even that he put a dime in the jukebox and sang "The Name Game" to me, whispering "Shirley Shirley Bo Birley" in my ear. Maybe all those things together made me decide to leave his hand there, when he slid it lower than it should have been as we danced. But maybe it was because that night was the first time that I could recall during my marriage that my heart did not ache in Harris's absence. I had never considered that there might be another possibility until that night, and something in that realization made me ask Tommy Jack back to my apartment. I wasn't the sort to even think about those things, let alone with a man a few years younger than me, and never had done anything like that before. I made him wait in the parking lot until Imogene went home. She gave me all the niceties—the kids had been good, had popcorn, went to bed on time, all that, and was probably confused when I rushed her out the door, but I did just the same, already inventing lies to tell the following day.

The next year of my life was filled with expectation, rather than longing. Harris was virtually always gone, and even when he was in town I don't know where he stayed. Most times it wasn't with us. Tommy Jack McMorsey had gotten a job as a long-haul truck driver, and he fudged his logbooks some, staying here for five days every two weeks. I have no idea how he got away with it, and I didn't care, as long as we were together. He spent a fair amount of that time with his war buddy, Fred, but most of it was with me. They shared something different that I had no connection to, but, then, so did we. The particulars aren't important, but we fell into a comfortable routine, where he would show up late on a Wednesday night and stay until Monday morning. It was maybe six months later when I admitted to myself that I had fallen in love and that I had never known that feeling before, not with Harris, anyway, and certainly not with anyone I had dated before Harris. What Harris and I felt was maybe love but love out of comfort and expectation. What Tommy Jack had was something else. It was as if some part of me that had been asleep my whole life had been awakened by Tommy Jack. When he was away, I felt like

48

that part of me was gone, some critical organ or limb, and I only felt complete after that when he was near, which is to say I felt incomplete fairly often. Our love was dictated by the limits of the lives we had chosen before we had awakened.

I never actually saw him off. Technically, he stayed at Fred's place, and that was where he left from. For me he was always just off somewhere busy, not really gone. It was the only way I could make it through the times when he was on the road or back at his home, sleeping and dreaming some eighteen hundred miles away, in a place I had never seen and likely never would. We made a sort of odd family in that period—Fred, his little boy, Tommy Jack, my five kids, and me. I think Fred missed Tommy Jack as much as I did when he was away. They would talk of the war when I was around, but sometimes in the middle of a conversation they would suddenly remember I was with them, and they would change the subject instantly. Those were conversations for their private time, the things they shared. For me it was like reading a book where some of the pages had been randomly ripped out. Martha Boans made herself scarce in those days, disapproving of the things I was doing. She had wound up in just as bad a marriage, but she chose to treat it as a virtue, proving how good a person she was to endure, bathing in her strength as the wife of a wandering drunk.

I never spent too much time on the reservation with Tommy Jack—that was a place for him and Fred—but we were visible enough in the city. Did people talk? I'm sure they did. Reservation gossip extends out to city Indians, too, eyes and ears everywhere, but Harris had been so consistently mean that no one told him. They liked it better that he had no idea what my life was like when he was gone. Fear or revenge, the reason behind the silence didn't matter. Maybe it was just indifference, since he was hardly around at all, anyway.

It might have seemed like I had little keeping me here, but the opposite was true, and that was something Tommy Jack never understood. Family extends out in all directions to and from you out here. It's a wonder any marriage works at all on the reservation, with the husband's family pulling him in one direction and the wife's family pulling her. I thought marrying Harris was a safe thing, since his family was so much farther away, but in the end all that meant was it took him longer to go there and longer to come back.

Tommy Jack spoke suddenly one night while we were lying together in the dark. "Fred says he cannot stay here. He's leaving. Gonna go to Hollywood he says. Wants to be an Indian star," Tommy Jack said, rolling over and looking at me in the moonlight.

"That's the craziest thing I ever heard of," I said. That Fred, always clowning around. The only acting experience he had was in front of my bay window, revealing truths and lies through the lips of strangers in light and shadow across a few silent city blocks. He was good-looking, I had to give him that. Not even one trace of Dick showed up in him, even as he aged. He was like a picture-book Indian, like he had fallen straight off a nickel or the side of an Iroquois Lager beer can, but even someone as uneducated as me knew it took more than good looks to get to Hollywood. And, besides, they weren't exactly making movies featuring real Indians then.

"What about that little boy? Is he taking him along? Who's gonna watch him out in Hollywood? This is the dumbest idea. Tommy Jack, you're pulling my leg." He reached over and slid his hand softly up my thigh.

"I am now, but about Fred? No, I wish I was, Darlin', but I am not. He says this place is killing him. Says he sees things, but he won't tell me what they are, and I do not ask. I see enough things of my own that I wish I couldn't. I do not need his, too." He rested his head on my shoulder, that bristly beard he was growing in scratching at me some. "He wants me to take the boy. Maybe even adopt him."

"And what do you know about raising kids? It's hard work, day and night, and particularly doing it alone. I know, I can tell you, and half the women on this reservation can tell you but not too many of the men. Tommy Jack, if you take that little boy, you're as dumb as Fred Howkowski. I ought to call him right this instant, and—"

"I was thinking I might not have to do it alone. I want you to come back with me to Texas."

I rolled over, pulling away from his touch, and we just went to sleep that night. We talked about it a few more times. I never brought it up, but my silence never stopped him. He didn't understand how hard it had been to leave the reservation in the first place and live in the city. Living more than an hour away would have been unbearable for me and my kids, for Harris and Barry too, any Indian I know. Fred wouldn't survive out there. But, anyway, the words to say this to Tommy Jack never came right, so I would just answer his invitation with whatever came into my head at that moment. I would force the words, fold them, so that they sounded like answers to his question, but they never really were, and he must have figured that out at some point because he stopped asking, and, as I said, he eventually just vanished, exactly the way Harris would: there one day, gone the next, without so much as a good-bye. Something had changed in his heart. Maybe it was the way Harris's

51

cousins had gotten after him. No one had told Harris, but some of his relatives had heard about that red-bearded man who was spending too much time with me, and they decided to take care of things on their own, jumping him one night in the dark, the way cowards do, but he was a tougher sort than that. A swelled nose and a shiner wouldn't scare that man off. It was something else, maybe even the fact that I was not about to leave New York with him, no matter how much I might love him.

I must have known it was coming at some point. One of the last times we were together, I had pulled out the camera, and, though most of the pictures I took were of my own kids and Fred, I had Tommy Jack and that little namesake boy pose in front of the truck. I had duplicates made of this roll of exposures and gave one to him and kept the other. That was in May, and by July he stopped showing up, and in August I had it confirmed. My old car was up on blocks behind Imogene's house, Fred Howkowski really had made it to Hollywood, the boy was gone, and Tommy Jack McMorsey was not coming back, no matter how much I might want him to.

Fred was gone for two more years before he came home again, and that second time it was for good. Since I had already experienced his death that night at the bowling alley, when it really came, it seemed not real, like I had heard that news three years before. Imogene called and asked me to come over, and, though she hadn't said why, I had a good idea. I had talked to Fred occasionally once he'd gotten to Hollywood, and I knew not only that things hadn't gone well for his dreams but also that he just wasn't right. I tried to not hear the strange things he said, knowing there was no way I could get out to Hollywood to rescue him from whatever was there. I had seen the bruises I suspected Dick had given him when he was a boy, so I had always let him stay with me, protecting him the only way I could, never speaking of those things. This time he was on his own, and for my part I failed him in every way possible.

He had a phone for a while, but it was eventually shut off. I wrote sometimes, but I never had much advice. Look at my life. How could I give someone anything to go on? I was too busy trying to fill the emptiness Tommy Jack had left. Harris had always left gradually. I could tell the itch was on him days before he disappeared, and I suppose I knew he would be back. After a month of Tommy Jack being gone and not answering his phone, I knew he wasn't coming back, and, besides, I had my own hands full by that time. I was pregnant with my last baby, Annie.

"Fred's no longer with us," Imogene said when I got to her place. I couldn't even for a second pretend she was merely stating the obvious, that he was in California. The postcards he had sent in his time there were spread out over the dinette, as if Imogene could arrange them in a certain way and they would have told her what happened or maybe how she could have prevented it, if she had just read them the right way.

"He's coming home on Tuesday. We have to go to the airport to get him. I had him burned. It wouldn't have been an open casket anyway," she said, before breaking down, dropping tears all over that oak veneer of hers.

"How did—" I started, but even I didn't how to finish that question. What did I want to know? Whatever happened didn't matter and neither did the way she found out.

"Tommy Jack called. He said he'd gotten a letter from Fred, telling him it would be too late to do anything but asking him to take care of things there in California. I suppose since he was the only one to go visit Fred he was the only one to know where to find him." That he committed suicide was apparent in the things Imogene refused to say, and, again, it didn't matter really. Dead is dead, no matter how you might try to cut it up and rearrange it. "Tommy Jack is taking care of things and having him sent home. He offered to drive Fred home, but I want him here as soon as possible." The broken glass that had been firmly wedged in my heart shifted in that instant. Tommy Jack had almost been back in my life again, and I would have taken it. Even under these terrible circumstances I would have silently celebrated. As that shard settled back down, Imogene moved it again. "So, we're gonna wait the service until Saturday. He can make it up here with the little boy by then."

Fred arrived home a couple of days later. I'd been prepared for his death since he'd been drafted, so that part wasn't quite so jarring. But it was still hard to believe that he'd survived Vietnam and all that mess, only to have the palm trees and big houses of Hollywood wind up being his end. I rode with Nora Page, and we drove Imogene and Dick to the airport to retrieve him. When I got in the backseat, I sat on something hard, and it turned out to be one of those plastic Indians all the kids were playing with those days. I know my kids had decided one of the plastic Indians was Fred, and I think that was probably true for most reservation kids as well.

I kept it out of sight on the side of me opposite of where Dick sat. He looked even older suddenly. Maybe all those whippings and beatings he had delivered came back to him as we worked our way home through traffic. I know how Dick is, and, even then, he probably thought he just hadn't done it enough. Maybe if he had beat Fred harder or more often, he would have toughened the boy up to the point that Hollywood would have been no trouble, and we'd be looking at Fred on the silver screen instead of in the little concrete box sitting between us. That small box didn't seem like it could possibly contain Fred, no matter how much I knew it to be. All that energy, all that life, all that laughter, none of it could fit in that little box.

BURYING VOICES

Fred Howkowski

Forgetting. That's what this is really about: trying to sort out those times in your experience with someone that you'd just as soon not have to carry around with you for the rest of your life. They tell you it's about remembering, when they try to sell your family the inspirational cards with your entry and exit dates and some moving verse, the guest book, the thank-you cards with matching envelopes, the obituary with the carefully worded language—in this case, "died suddenly"—the urn, the nameplate, the concrete sealer. That one is a harder sell on the reservation. It's required by law most places but not at home. We don't mind that our dead grow back into the earth, so the man in the black suit and sedate tie tries to apply the laws of physics to my family's grief, not knowing his pitch ensures the exact opposite reaction. He suggests that the back hoe is heavy, and, if the newly turned earth sinks at the wrong time, my urn could crack open under all that pressure, and then I'd be spilling out all over the place. Those white people, they think that's a bad thing, but, once all the people from home get me in place, they know their jobs.

These suspension straps lower me into the hole then slide out from under me, and the last ritual begins. They want to pretend they're helping to bury me, my last mortal remains, but what they really drop down into this deep hole are memories, unwanted, muddy thickly clotted memories, laced with roots and worms and beetles, the occasional termite.

My father is first. I recognize his hand immediately. He lets the dirt fall in hard clumps, hitting the top of my urn. I wonder if he's using two hands to pick up a large enough chunk. He's looking to make a dent, leave a mark, anything. Here we are, when I'm seven, and we get our first TV, and he lets me know, as soon as my mother leaves the room, that I am not to tell my friends we have one, since he doesn't want his house filled up with TV-less Indians, who should be out looking for jobs, anyway, instead of watching his TV, and he even closes the front curtains when he has it on, so no one can see its glow, as if that large metal antenna on the roof didn't give our situation away, and here we are at my eleventh birthday, when he hands me a three-pack of rubbers and tells me to keep these in my wallet at all times because you never know when opportunity is going to knock, and I better not even think about knocking some girl up because we can't afford to feed even one more mouth, let alone two, and here we are, when I let him know I've been drafted and am soon to be a father myself, that it's clear the thing that troubles him more is not that I'll be taking lives and risking my own but that I'll be bringing a new one into the world. Maybe those are enough memories for him to get rid of at this moment. I'm sure he doesn't want to linger inappropriately, so he'll be back later.

My mother is second and even a little unsteady in the way she tosses the dirt in. She sprinkles it like she would powdered sugar on top of fry bread on occasion. She doesn't want to give up that many memories, but I know the ones she's dusting me with. They are those last few weekends I come home on leave, saving all my pay so I can get back here, and she grows more and more busy every time I return. That last time she asks me not to come back, that it's too hard to see me leave, and I can see she'll be relieved when I head out for Vietnam for good, so she can begin the forgetting process in earnest. She's been rehearsing for this minute going on five years.

My little brother, Gary Lou, holds her hand and tosses his own handful in, small clumps of memory, mostly fear. And here we are, me yelling for my gun from my room in the middle of every night, and he remembering mostly that he wishes I never came home, so he wouldn't have to experience this stranger sleeping in the next room, this stranger who's wearing his brother's face. He's holding onto all those other memories, the ones of the brother he knew before. He's not giving a one of them up.

And here's Nadine Waterson, sinking the heels of those fierce "come jig me" shoes she wears on a Saturday night. She kicks some clumps in and grabs one big chunk to toss my way. And here we are when she tells me the boy isn't even likely mine but that I can have him if I want. She's wanting me to be pissed, hurt, anything, and it's her own disappointment that she dumps here, when she realizes that I don't care, as long as he has a chance at a good life. She'll rewrite this one so that I'm the sucker after all, and she's free to do so.

And Martha Boans comes along in her prim dress, not black exactly, gray, maybe it had been black at some point. And here we are, at her table, and she's asking me why I brought that awful man back with me who's been ruining Shirley's reputation. And here we are after I say Shirley's a big girl and can make her own decisions. I guess, if Martha can make that conversation go away, she thinks she can make Tommy Jack himself go away.

And Shirley Mounter finally steps up. She's been circling through this crowd, coming close to the hole, stepping back, moving between people, but finally she chooses a firm clod and breaks it in two. She gives up precious little. She drops in one piece from the clump in her hand and tosses the other back to the mound, as if others won't pick up that piece. And here we are when I tell her on the phone that the little people are following me all around Los Angeles, that they're trying to protect me, the way they have protected lost Indians forever, but that I see them less and less, that even the little people are giving up on me and returning to the reservation to protect more deserving souls—this is what she tosses to me. The piece she throws back to the mound I can't see, but we both know what it is—her silence on the other end of the line during that last telephone conversation, her eternal silence.

And my little boy comes up next, but he doesn't have much to drop, very little to spare. He gives one up, a token, because he already knows rituals are expected of him. He chooses well. And here we are, me walking away in the Lubbock airport terminal and he refusing to wave as I step out that door and into a different life.

And Tommy Jack, he steps up and looks down on me as he had hundreds of times over there, in the jungles. I was always clumsier than him, so, when we shared a foxhole, he made me jump in first, since he could always jump in second and not step on me. He holds the dirt up to his face, breathes deep, knows the scent of earth around me. Over there we rubbed the dirt on each other's faces, trying, always trying, to disappear. He smudges some into his beard and then lets it drop on me and steps back. The only time he wants to give. And here we are, in my apartment in Los Angeles, but I can't see all that well, because I have blown a significant part of my head off and he doesn't want to look, but he does. He identifies me. And here we are.

And others come, dropping careless pieces, dismissing all memories, good and bad, playing fireball, drinking, shooting pool, pickup basketball games, me throwing up at some party, people who will just vaguely remember me in a year and only as a momentary flash after that. And here they are, disposing of me as only they can.

And here I am, home. And here I am. Home.

Part Two Cutting Patterns

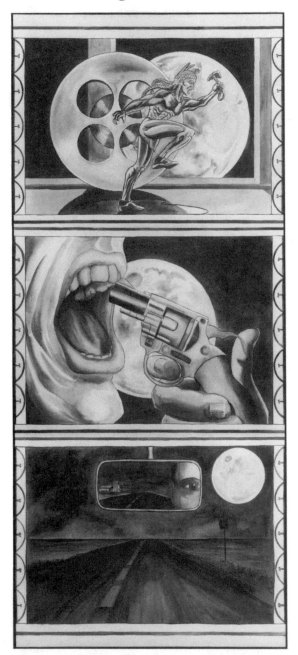

Chapter 4 Leaving Messages

T. J. Howkowski 1984

Liza Jean McMorsey was the kind of woman who could forgive a million lies but could never forgive the truth. Lies were much easier to fit into her china cabinet type of world, where people remained static, caught in a moment in their lives, like the porcelain figures she collected so feverishly. She even insisted I call her Momma after the formal adoption, though she and my adoptive daddy decided I should keep my real last name. She took comfort in the fictional world we made for ourselves here, in the flat-lands of Texas, where she and Daddy grew up. I wound up here, after my real daddy passed me on and headed to Hollywood. Then he went and killed himself a year later, totally nuts after surviving Vietnam, only to fail at the one thing he had wanted in his life. Since I was named Tommy Jack, after her husband, I suspicion she didn't want me thinking I was officially a "junior" to him. She wanted me to always know I was definitely an adopted child. When I told Daddy that I was going to carry on and do what my real daddy couldn't succeed at and that I was going to do it the right way, he about went up the wall.

He had been saving money for my college education since he took me on as his own when I was five, but he informed me last year that, if I were enrolling in acting school, then I would be doing it solo. He refused to contribute a single penny to that nonsense. Fortunately, he said that in enough time for me to try different avenues, and by the time they left me, picking up shards of broken glass and porcelain while they made their way to the cabin in New Mexico, I already had plans firmly in place.

I walked down to the Allslip's a few miles away and left lighter ten minutes later, a pocketful of quarters traded for electrical impulses, my voice, crossing all those pay phone miles to the reservation in New York and my pen pal cousin, Brian Waterson. When I first moved to Texas, Daddy wanted to give me some kind of connection with my old home and family, and maybe it should have said something to me that the only one he found who was willing to keep in touch was a kid about my own age.

Brian was a reservation kid, had spent his whole life there. It was the right thing, Brian agreeing to do me this favor. Through the years he would write of things he was doing, the usual reservation kid things, I suppose, but to me they were the only doorway. Through him I could be at the Border Crossing Celebration, the National Picnic, fireball games. The real reservation became only a foggy memory for me, but the new one, in my head, held vast adventures with my cousin and all those other kids he was connected to. He had always been a good letter writer and was in college, trying to become a reporter for the newspapers. He was going to show me the ropes of college in the fall, anyway, but, since he was on summer vacation and hadn't started his internship yet, he was free for about a week, just enough time to give me the major assist I needed.

He guessed, looking at maps, that it would take probably four days to get here. Daddy, driving the big rigs for a living, used to make it in less time than that, but four days was fine. I would be ready by the time Brian got to Texas. I told him not to call, no matter what. I would see him when he arrived. By the time I made it back from the pay phone, the sun had begun to set, and the rooms had grown dark.

Packing was easy. I had planned it out through much of my senior year, gradually selecting those things I would need to survive up there in New York. All my clothes that still had pretty decent wear in them were the first things I separated out. Most of the toys and junk that remained from my childhood I had already stored in boxes in the basement, so it was just a matter of moving them to the Yorkston House before I left, and Brian could help me with those things when he rolled into town.

"Howdy!" my voice yelled from our answering machine, "none of us is here, right now, so just let us know which one of us y'all's looking for and a number we can hook y'all up at. Thanks," my voice said. People frequently say they hate the way their voices sound on tape, that they don't sound anything like the way they hear themselves. One of the first acting class homework assignments I got was to record my voice, reading a paragraph, and to play it back over and over until I grew accustomed to hearing my voice without cringing. My teacher said you cannot gauge your performance until you have acclimated yourself to hearing a stranger's voice and recognizing it as your own and accepting that fact. Only then could you be objective. I had mastered that fairly well, but, when our answering machine kicked in, I no longer recognized the voice coming from that speaker. It belonged to a different guy, one who used to live here.

That guy was smart enough to know how to lie. That guy was the one who could bring home a gift for his momma, purchased on the road trip he and his daddy had just come home from, knowing that his daddy had spent the night in the company of another. That guy knew how to keep both of those parents happy. That guy would have never told his momma that his daddy had married her only because the woman he really loved was not ever going to be available. That guy would have never heard the only woman he'd known as a mother say, "Goddamned Indians always sticking together, like a bunch of fucking cockroaches." That guy would have known better than to get that kind of reaction. That guy would have known which things to say and which things to keep still about. That guy would have been afraid of the costs and unwilling to pay them. I was pretty sure that guy was not coming back, ever, and, even if he did, there would be no one who would receive him.

Each time my old voice invited a message, Daddy's voice came through in reply, worse and worse. The first message was just awkward, with lots of background noise. Given the time, he was at the Midway Diner and Truck Stop in Tatum, where we always got the steak fingers and gravy, an extra order if we were on the way home from a long haul, to bring home to Momma, to join whatever porcelain figurine we had found for her, along the way. Behind his voice NancyJo, the waitress with too much blue eye shadow, flirted for higher tips with horny, sweaty truck drivers, being just suggestive enough to make a living wage. I always wondered what she did when her shift was over, where she lived, if there were kids at home, watching TV, depending on her ability to arouse desperate, bored men on their way to somewhere else. "Boy," my daddy's voice told the answering machine, "you know where the credit card is, in the top right desk drawer, in that last dark envelope. Just don't be foolish with it. And you know where the truck keys are, same thing there, but I know you're a good boy. I'll call when I can and let you know when Momma has cooled down some. You know you shouldn't have said those things, but that can't be helped now."

The second call would have been from Roswell, where all the weirdos hang out, looking for aliens as much as they were looking for men. There the stop would have been Area 51 Gas and Diesel. He only stopped there if we were really drowsy or really hungry or needed to fill the tanks. Too high a percentage of what Daddy called the "odd trade," women who, when you met them, you never knew what you were in for. "Boy, it looks like it's going to be a while, good thing we got you that license when we did. You been on the road a good enough number of years now, you know to be careful. It is not good enough that you know how to be safe yourself, remember that. Always watch out for the other drivers and the unexpected turns. I will try to get back to check on you as I can. No later than July, for sure. Maybe we can get you out here before the big Independence Day block party. The one thing we got going for us is that your momma surely knows folks'll be asking after your whereabouts, if you ain't here by then, and she's not likely to want to share all those details. Anyway, nothing definite yet. I'll see what I can do about getting my routes changed, once I check in with dispatch in Cascabel."

In the basement where my suitcases had been stored, I found the leftover paint and spackle we kept around for when Momma decided to engage in those elaborate redecorating fits she was occasionally taken with. I filled in the holes from where she missed me in throwing those figurines and got the walls instead, and, by the time I started sanding them, the third call came in. "Boy, whatever else happens, I will be there to help you leave for school in August. And the money I had saved for your college? It's in a savings account in your name in the right-hand top drawer. I had it all set up to surprise you with. Go on and take it. Don't you worry now. I'll do what I can to help you, but, well, for now don't call me, I'll call you." He must have been in Cascabel by that time, maybe calling from the consignment place he sold junk out of. In the drawer the passbook sat right where he said it was, thirty thousand dollars penned in the opening deposit slot, in his messy handwriting. I have no idea how he had saved that much, but there it was, with an official bank deposit receipt. I slid it back in place, exactly as I had found it.

I went to bed around midnight, figuring he wouldn't call any later. Not because he wouldn't be up but because he wouldn't have any more excuses to leave the cabin, and I imagine he was probably running a little short on quarters, though he always kept a ridiculous number of them in his jeans pockets.

Over the next couple days I gradually got the house back in order, cleaned up the shards, repainted the walls, stacked all of my belongings on the back stoop, and was down to the last few steps before leaving when my cousin Brian pulled in. He was even a little earlier than I expected, and the trip made clear weary marks on him, all eighteen hundred miles worked into his rumpled look as he slowly climbed from the pickup.

"So, which house?" he asked, which only seemed odd until I remembered the variety of houses I had seen on the reservation.

"These boxes," I said, pointing to the stack, "go over into that house, and the last few, over there, go with us. Don't you want to rest? Something to drink?"

"Yeah, a pop would be good," he said, looking over the boxes and the descriptions I had written on them. "We're moving some of this stuff just across the driveway?" He guzzled the root beer down in two chugs. I picked up the first box, carried it into the Yorkston House, and headed up the staircase. He followed with another box.

Daddy and I had, with some help, refurbished the Yorkston House after he'd had it dragged to our place from a farm two roads over. Some of it had been burnt out, but most of the key structural boards had remained intact. The house movers couldn't understand why he was willing to pay all that money to drag a semi-burnt-out house from an old cotton field, but they took his money anyway. They laughed and dropped the Yorkston place down on the opposite side of the driveway from our house, hauling ass before Daddy could have a change of mind. But he was never going to change his mind. He isn't that kind of man. Once Daddy has something in his head, it sits there and builds a nest, just like a sparrow does. You can tear it out and tear it out, but the sparrow will keep onto that place it chose no matter what, and that is just how ideas were in my daddy's old brain.

He could see what Big Antler had once looked like. While he made his living as a long-haul trucker, he had started out as a history buff, finishing a master's degree in history before deciding he didn't want to live his life in a classroom, after all. Still, he just loved living in Big Antler, and we spent almost every weekend chasing down fragments of the past at estate sales and garage sales, to resell at his junk store booth. If anything we came across had clearly come from the German settlers around the town, he just hung onto that.

Eventually, Momma said he had crowded their house with too much junk. She was a collector, too, but of more refined things than he was, beaded purses and art deco accessories as well as the figurines. She saw no place for a galvanized bathtub or a straight-blade cabbage shredder in her house, and he had two choices, get rid of them or put them in storage. Just about that time old man Yorkston had died, owing Daddy's family a bit of money. The Yorkston kids didn't want that old house anymore, so they gave it to Daddy, if he wanted to move it. So, that summer the Yorkston place rolled down the road bathed in caution lights then landed at our place.

After he had some skilled carpenters do structural work, Daddy and I spent most of that summer reinventing the inside. He found some old wallpaper samples in the attic, and we hunted down some similar ones to do the place up in. It was then mostly a matter of moving all his local antiques into the house and deciding where they should go. When we were done, the place looked almost as if the residents had decided one day, fifty or so years in the past, to just up and leave, walk out the door—frying pan on the stove, Quaker Oats in the cupboard, Vick's Vapo-Rub on the medicine shelf, magazines on the coffee table, all just waiting for the people to come back and make them useful again. It was in this place that I found a home. The regular house was very much Momma's, the road was Daddy's place, and the reservation a place I invented, filtered through Brian's letters, but the Yorkston House had come to me clean, and it was filled with things I had helped find along the way. We rebuilt a past. It wasn't my past necessarily, but its current arrangement I was at least involved with. Whenever I felt most alone, I went to the Yorkston House and sat in the rocking chair or lay on the sofa until the feeling passed, and then I could go back into the orderly universe Momma had designed for herself while Daddy and I wandered the country's veins in his rig.

"This is creepy, man. What is up with that stepfather of yours?" Brian asked, dropping a box of books beside me on the planks of the upstairs floor.

"Not a stepfather. He adopted me," I said.

"Well, whatever, this is still just not right, man. It's like that *Twilight Zone* episode, where the people wander into that abandoned town, come to find out it's a toy town for a giant kid, and suddenly they're trapped. Remember that one?" Brian looked around in the dim light. I had switched the Yorkston House's electricity on, but the few lights really did little for the gloomy interior. "World War Over," he read from a headline of one of the newspapers lining the upstairs walls.

"Yeah, that was how they lined and insulated their walls back then, newspapers. We went a long way to get everything right, even using newspapers from the right era," I said.

"Okay, so, why are we moving your stuff up here, anyway? You moving into this house? Man, this would really freak me out if I lived here. Swear, I would be seeing ghosts every night. This reminds me of my grams's house."

"Well, are you scared there?" I asked.

"No. It's my grams's house. She's just that way. Can't ever throw anything away, so everything becomes a part of her place."

"Well, that's how this is, except my daddy's doing it for a whole town instead of just himself. He even does tours for school kids, or whoever, if they can catch him in town."

"Really?"

"Yup."

"Okay, but that still doesn't tell me why we're doing this."

"Just go grab another box, while I make room here in the attic," I said, prying the door above the staircase loose. The crawlspace was dark and warm, a perfect environment for brown recluses and scorpions, but I had sealed up all of my boxes. I just had to be careful shifting all the junk already up there.

"You want help moving that stuff?" Brian asked a few minutes later, climbing the stairs with another box. "I'm skinnier than you are, and maybe I can just hop up inside that cubby, and you can hand me the boxes."

"No, just bring them over, that'll be great. And don't kill yourself. You aren't used to this heat. Take a break whenever you need. There's more soda in the outside fridge, just help yourself," I said, and slid the first three boxes of my life in Texas deep into the dark spaces within the Yorkston House, where they faded into the quiet history of an old farm-house in west Texas. I was not sure if I would ever see my belongings again, so I left them in the only place I could almost call my own.

(((

"You want me to get that?" Brian asked, when the phone rang early the next morning.

"No, don't." I said. We listened to the old me give instructions to incoming callers and then to my daddy's new voice, which seemed to grow more and more faint with each call he made back here.

"Boy, call me when you get these messages. Just call the cabin, let it ring once, then hang up, and I will call you right back," he said, paused, like he was about to say something else, then hung up.

"That him?"

"Yup."

"You guys sound alike. You gonna call him back?" I shook my head and went to get dressed, strip the bedding in my room, and wash it. "What time you wanna leave?" Brian asked, throwing his sheets in.

"Just a couple things left to do," I said, stepping to the stack of photos I had removed from the walls two days before, popping the frame from the first and sliding the picture out. "Then we can go. You wanna help with this? Or make coffee, whatever, eat some breakfast." I lifted the next picture and did the same thing.

"Sure, I'll help you, but what are we doing?" he said, picking the next frame up, sliding the photo from it, and setting the frame and picture into the two separate piles I was making.

"Here, look at this," I said, walking to their bedroom closet and moving a few shoe boxes to reveal a slightly bigger box behind them. "My daddy showed this to me once, years ago. I suspect maybe as a way to keep me in line or to show what we had to lose if I were to spill some particular beans on him."

"I don't get it," he said. "Who's the guy cut out of all these pictures? I mean, wouldn't it have been easier to just cut most of these pictures in half? Then you could still have a nice picture." He passed them back to me, these photos of my adoptive mother in a variety of settings. There she was in a nice sweater, in front of a hearty fireplace fire, and leaning against the rails of some boat, in a party with several members of her family, dancing at some reception, and in each of these a tall man's headless body stood near her, sometimes holding on, sometimes just standing there. In each photo nothing else was altered. His head was neatly cut around the borders, and, if you looked closely, you could see he was a blond man, but, other than that, his features were entirely unknown to me.

"My momma's first husband. I guess she wanted to remember him this way, not wiped out entirely, just enough to know that the end had been a conscious decision. When I first moved here, she even had one up on the wall at her house, but, when she moved in with us, all those pictures disappeared. I had wondered what happened to them, and one day my daddy showed them to me."

"Had you asked him?"

"No, well, you see, my daddy had a way with women and . . . it's not important."

"Yeah, some people from home still remember that reputation."

"Really?"

"Yup, and that's probably not a good thing."

"Well, it wasn't a good thing here, either. I guess I knew some things about him that, well, I knew he maybe shouldn't have been doing those things, but I also got to know how to keep my mouth shut, too. And these pictures were a big part of that. And you and me, well, we're just making sure my head doesn't wind up in a basket somewhere." He nodded, and we continued to separate pictures from frames.

"Where were all these, anyway?" he asked, as we got to the last.

"On the walls, there, in the hall. I spackled over and painted where they were. You can probably tell if you look close enough, but it'll do. I got pretty handy working on the Yorkston House. Never enough to be a professional but enough to get by."

"You taking them with you?"

"Uh-uh, come on. I'll show you." We collected the photos and walked them out to the pump house and over to the shelf where another important box of secrets had rested all these years without my even knowing it. "Hang onto these," I said, flipping the light switch.

The recently disturbed box was back in its place, not even inches from the dusty space it kept on the shelf. The other box, the one containing the secret of my daddy's long-standing love for Shirley Mounter, was gone for good. Where Momma took it several days before, when she first found out about its existence from my big mouth, I have no idea. I also have no idea if Daddy will ever forgive me for the loss of those things he had hidden for so many years. She was only gone for about twenty minutes when she took it all away, but, even in a town as small as Big Antler, I would have no idea where I should begin looking. It wasn't even worth thinking about. I hoped Daddy had enough memories that he didn't really need those things after all, but I also know, particularly now, the power mementos can have over you.

I opened the remaining box, there on the shelf, and set the photos inside, on top of the North Vietnamese Army flag and the dented can of beer, from the days my two daddies spent together in the war, and some other things that I didn't recognize, a few boxes of stuff, a canister, some airmail letters. I had looked through this box fully, for the first time, late on the night they left, and set it back on the shelf, where it belonged. It had not contained what I'd hoped—the letter my real daddy had written to me, just before he shot himself, but there was something else in the box from that time. Or I assumed it was. No way to be sure without asking, and that did not seem like a good time to be making any telephone inquiries. I pulled it from the box.

"We aren't taking that, Tom. It's totally illegal."

"T.J."

"T.J.?"

"That's my name, that's what people call me now."

"Are you kidding?"

"No, I am not kidding."

"Well, don't expect me to get used to that fast. I've been calling you Tom since we first started that corny pen pal cousins stuff, what, ten years ago?"

"Eleven. Well, that's what I intend to be going by from now on."

"No promises, no guarantees."

"That's for sure. Well, I'm gonna take this into the house, anyway." We turned around, but, before I shut off the light, I changed my mind about one thing. "Here, reach back into that box and pull the top picture from the pile," I said.

《 《 《

"So, is that really it?" Brian asked, over a bowl of cereal, as we sat at the kitchen counter where I had eaten breakfast for years.

"Gotta be, I imagine. Everything else in that box belonged to him. Why not this?"

"Just seems kind of, I don't know, gruesome."

"Look, it's not loaded. Maybe the police kept the bullets when they handed it over, or maybe he was a sure shot, knew he didn't need a second one." The revolver's chambers were orange with rust, and its moving parts didn't turn with any grace whatsoever—though, frankly, I am not much for guns, so don't know how it's supposed to feel.

"You don't usually get a chance at a second shot, even if you weren't entirely successful."

"How about if we put it up under the dash or something? I have to take it." I don't know, maybe it was because this was the very last thing he had touched while he was still alive, that his body heat rode out into the Los Angeles air through the metal of this trigger. I would never shoot it, but I couldn't leave it here, knowing I might never be back this way.

"Yeah, okay, we'll put it somewhere. Maybe that is the best place, or maybe under the jack. We'll figure something out. Is that it? You about ready?" Brian washed his cup and set it in the cupboard.

"Just a second," I said. I walked through the rooms, I guess, trying to accumulate their details, seeing the places I could not erase myself from, as much as I had tried. The traces were small. No one else would notice them, but I would know they were there. In the bathroom Daddy and I shared, the Formica countertop was nicked, where I had slipped coming out of the shower and hit my mouth, losing one of my baby teeth. It was unlikely they'd replace that anytime soon.

The telephone rang one more time. Brian struggled with not answering it, but he knew I could tackle him if need be. "Boy," my daddy said, "just call when you get this, okay? I'll deal with it from this end." The noise in the background told me he was still not calling from home, and, if he wasn't brave enough to do that, he was for sure not going to be brave enough to make any difference in the current directions our lives were taking.

"You really should call him," Brian said. After a few minutes he nodded and picked up the revolver. "I'll see what I can do about a place for this. Just come out when you're ready, no hurry."

No hurry. That may have been so, but I had almost nothing holding me here anymore, either. A few permanent scars in the house's makeup—that was it. I did the last thing I was prepared to do. The one frame I needed sat waiting in the study. I slid the photograph back into it and bent the brackets into place. Daddy's hammer was where he always kept it, in that little toolbox near the washing machine, and the nails he used for hanging pictures were right there, too. I dragged my hand down the newly smooth hallway walls, leaving streaky prints, I imagined, but only the kind detectives would have to pick up with their little powder kits for crime scenes. About halfway down the hallway I stopped and nailed one small-headed nail in, neatly breaking the skin of my new paintjob.

The picture looked funny up on the wall all by itself. It almost dared Momma to get out her scissors, but I suspect Daddy would not let that happen, no matter the cost. The picture was a simple one, him and me, in front of his rig. I was about five years old, and the picture was taken when I wasn't even his boy yet. I sat up on the big chrome bumper, and he leaned against the grill. It was the only picture I've ever seen in which he was not wearing a cap of some sort or another, aside from those formal portrait studio ones Momma occasionally forced him into. His bright red hair stood up in a rooster tail in the early morning breeze. It appeared that he was bareheaded because I was wearing his cap, though it swamped my little boy's head, and I could only see from below it by lifting the bill with my hand.

Pictures are worth those thousand words, they say. This one was, anyway. Sometimes those thousand were the truth, sometimes not, and sometimes they fell in the middle somewhere. Daddy always said my real daddy took this picture of us, early one morning in May of that last year I lived in New York. Back then Daddy used to drive the rig from Texas to New York as his regular route, but it wasn't to see his best friend from the war. It was to see someone else, the person who had really taken this picture. Back then I didn't know why the two of them were always together, didn't think a thing of it. I spent a lot of time with her kids, since she and my real daddy had been good friends, and this was just one more person, as far as I was concerned. One who bought us ice cream and took us to the movies and who made everyone laugh whenever he would appear. It seemed like everyone just could not wait for him to pull back into our lives every couple weeks.

The picture was taken in May, early morning, but the long shadow, reaching out and touching us, belonged to Shirley Mounter and no one else. My real daddy was there that morning, I remember it well. The two men had just finished telling me I was maybe going to live with Tommy Jack for a while, so Daddy could head on out west and be a star. My world had finally come to be settled when my real daddy had gotten home from the war, taking me from the crazy woman who was my real momma, and here they were, suddenly tearing it up again. I could not stop crying, but they told me I should be a good boy for Shirley, and they pointed to her just then pulling into our driveway. She knew I had been crying, my eyes were all puffy, but she wanted to get this picture anyway. She asked my daddy to take that damned cap off so she could see his pretty hair, and he blushed for her but took it off anyway. He gripped the cap as she held the camera up to her face and then lowered it again.

"Put that cap on that poor little boy, or everyone will be wondering what he's crying his eyes out about," she said, "for years and years to come." He popped it on my head. It went down over my nose, and they laughed, and, when I lifted it up so I could see, I laughed too, to be with them, and in that moment she pressed that button and froze us there.

⟨ ⟨ ⟨

I put the hammer back where I had gotten it, slid our barstools back under the kitchen counter, and set the timer lights, like

I always did when we left for Cascabel. I went outside and cut the water in the pump house and looked at that box of my real daddy's possessions one last time, but I decided against taking them. Somehow, those things belonged here, in ways that I no longer did, ways I never truly had, I suppose. The backdoor lock turned easily with my key, and I slid the key from my ring and put it in my wallet, in the same secret pocket where I keep my real momma's address and phone number, just in case, always just in case. The phone rang as I got into Brian's truck, watching the shadows grow long on the York-ston House. My old voice probably delivered its tired old message as we pulled out of the driveway and headed east, the revolver secured under the jack.

Chapter 5 Identifying Marks

Annie Boans 1993

My husband, Doug, and my brother Royal were shooting a game of cutthroat when T. J. Howkowski made eye contact from across the room and walked over. I wondered when he had gotten back into town and why no one knew it. Perhaps I was the only one not to know it. The last time I had seen him was sometime in the mid-eighties. Brian Waterson would bring him out to the reservation for the National Picnic, the fireball game, things like that. I don't think most people our ages knew him at all, but a lot of the older generation did. That was when my interest in Fred Howkowski had been reawakened. I think he'd been dead for almost five years when I first took an interest. It would have been easy for my mother merely to say he'd died in the war, and that was perhaps accurate in its own way. It seemed like the country lost many things in that war, even those who stayed here, only catching versions of the truth in news coverage and in the later clarifications hidden in night whispers of those who came home and in the empty places of those who didn't.

I'd always been a quick study, a "smart one," is what they say on the reservation. I looked up everything I could. I recall being so angry in those few years before I could read, conducting research before I knew the word. I would stare at those words on the page, recognize the occasional one, try to force understanding, and, once I could read, I went after any possible thing I could find. By the time I was seven I was well informed of the ingredients of everything we ate, and I knew all the side effects and dosage instructions for every bottle in our medicine cabinet. I looked for new words everywhere, sneaking them from others' lips and into my ears. "Did you hear that Mitch Natcha got arrested for insulting his wife down at the Circle Club last night?" I said casually sitting on the step stool in the kitchen of our apartment, where my mother was having coffee with Martha Boans, Imogene Howkowski, and Nora Page. I'd heard my mother earlier that morning spreading some news by phone and wanted to try out my new words.

"Ha!" Martha said, laughing out a lungful of smoke. "I bet Tracy's wishing that insulted was all that happened to her last night. Eighteen stitches, from what I hear."

"Nineteen," Nora said.

"That's 'assaulted,' Babygirl, not insulted. It means getting beat up, and you shouldn't be telling such stories. Now go and play, while we have a visit," Imogene said, folding the step stool out from under me and sliding it next to the fridge. She touched my shoulders and pointed me to the doorway. In retrospect I can see how Imogene knew the ways of stories and how they could grow around you, creeping into your life until they were so mixed into the things you did that to tear them out would be like ripping at some vague growth on your body, only to discover it was a piece of your nervous system, reaching out to touch others because you had refused to for so long.

From that point my vocabulary only grew exponentially. I relished being the only person in the room to know things. My mother, though, felt I occasionally needed a little uncertainty in my life. At fourteen, when some days all we ate were lettuce and mayonnaise sandwiches, I wondered if my father were ever going to materialize with a sense of responsibility and some support money. While we waited, I worked my way through the set of encyclopedias my mother had bought on installments that was outdated before she made the last payment. At the close of the last book, two years later, I believed I knew everything in the world, and I made the error of sharing this belief with my mother.

Several days later she borrowed a car and drove me slowly through the reservation, pointing to dogs everywhere we went, asking what kind they were. I'd made a show early in my encyclopedia career of naming every dog on the color plate section of dog breeds, with the key hidden. I, of course, couldn't name a single dog I saw that day, and, as I grew frustrated and surly, my mother said quietly that life was never as simple as pure breeds. When we got home, she showed me select pages from a scrapbook she kept, including reports of the Kennedys getting shot and Martin Luther King, the Beatles breaking up, that capsule breaking out of the atmosphere for the first time and the Moon walk, the end of the war, all of these bullets flying through the sky, adding pieces to our world after our set of faux-leather-bound books were written and before I had cultivated awareness, and then I got some perspective again.

I hadn't remembered Fred Howkowski at all, had only a vague notion he'd been part of my family's history, but it was an intangible part, as far as I was concerned. Royal remembered him more than our other siblings, but he refused to divulge. He withheld all sorts of information like that, at his whim. This lack of information sharing was a source of pride for him. There were few things he had that I didn't, and he had no intention of giving them up carelessly. I pestered him with particular enthusiasm one day, and, finally, he sighed and spoke quietly. "Fred Howkowski gave the biggest 'fuck you' to the world, and that included us, so I ain't having any part of that conversation, ever. So, you should just forget about asking me again."

Our family photo albums contained myriad pictures of Fred, from childhood to adolescence. Most were taken in our old apartment, the one in which my mother still lived. Additionally, we had a few from his Vietnam era. In these Fred was usually accompanied by a man sporting a bushy red mustache. On one of the rare occasions Royal willingly answered a question, he said the man was "just some white guy Fred used to know," which, while technically true, was hardly half the story. I later pieced together that this was the man raising Fred's son, somewhere in the Southwest. There had to be so much more to the story than that. Royal wouldn't budge, however, and the few times I'd asked my mother about the other man in the picture, or about Fred himself for that matter, such grave sadness overtook her that I couldn't bear to broach the topic again. She said minor things, relatively useless, that he was nice and funny and gentle, but her responses took so much out of her, I resisted the urge to further explore until it came time for college, when I discovered very little had been done on the relationship between Indian actors and their inclusion in American film. While probably a rationalization for my own nosiness, I felt a duty to explore the story of Fred Howkowski guilt-free, and that suited me fine, but I was to discover precious little existed of his career. That discovery was deeply frustrating until I realized the absence itself was worthy of exploration, and absence is something with which I am highly familiar.

Doug and I begin our anniversary every year with a confirmation and reminder that absence lurks around every corner, unexpectedly waiting to come to the forefront, nearly a tangible thing itself. This year was no different. We would run into T. J. Howkowski a little later in the evening, but the festivities began, as they always did, on top of the reservoir, where Doug handed me his anniversary gift.

"So, do you like it?" He waited, smiling, as I turned his gift over in my hands, the bottle opener in the shape of a Lakota chief's head, smiling at me. Though I refused to admit it, the little thing suited me, and perhaps it should have illustrated how my husband truly did love me, but it was not the sort of thing I was expecting. It was so repulsive that I'd even thought I had lost it a little later in the evening, but Royal had snagged it while I hadn't been looking, and, ultimately, I had forgotten it by that time.

"Sure, of course, mostly because you gave it to me, but, yeah, it'll be a neat addition to the collection." Doug knew what I was saying, had years of translations under his belt, and he knew he was not likely to have as good an anniversary as he'd expected. That was truly the case for everyone celebrating with us, and only the smallest part was because of his bad choice in gifts. Those kinds of issues diminish quickly.

"And useful, too, don't forget useful. Speaking of which—"

"So, why do we always have to come here on our anniversary?" I asked, opening a fresh beer for Doug with the new opener and then, considering, opened another for myself. "Royal? Pierce? Gracie? You guys ready?" I asked, holding the case open.

"Because this is the place you come to remember all the things you cherish and how easy you can lose them," Doug said, slowly, as if he were explaining things to an especially dense child. "You of all people should know that. It was losing the land under this dike that caused your ma and dad to move away."

"And your ma and dad to buy our house, don't forget that part of it," Royal interrupted, as was his tendency.

". . . and all of you guys to grow up as a bunch of city Indians," Doug finished, unfazed, accustomed to Royal's frequent editorial insertions.

"City Indians," I said, "you make us sound like something totally different from you guys who grew up out here."

"You are," Doug responded.

"Well, that was romantic. Why did I ever marry you?" I opened the beers, flipping the caps with the new opener.

"My killer braiding skills? Or maybe some of my other skills? After all, this was also the first place we ever—"

"The braiding, definitely the braiding," I laughed, and then reached back and smoothed my hair. "You do have a way." I rolled over and looked at the sky. "You think we'll ever move back here?"

"Think you could handle it?"

"What's to handle?"

"Different way of life, Miss Indian Artist," Royal said, from his place on the hood of his Chevelle.

"That's Ms. Indian Art Historian. Get it straight," I said, squinting at him in the late-afternoon sunlight. "You better be nice to me, or I won't let you crash on our couch when you get too drunk to drag your car home. It's a sacrifice, you know, the way you always pass gas on it and that damn smell stays for days."

"Pass gas, she says. How polite. Be thankful that farting is all I do, little sister." Royal walked over to the case and examined the gift. "Cool opener, Dougie, where'd you get it?"

"The shop."

"Jeez, I didn't see any, and I was there all afternoon."

"Well, if you'd actually spend the time working, you would have seen them, right there on the counter in front of you," Doug said, revealing that he was sometimes like his mother.

"You got my anniversary gift at the smoke shop?" I asked, with more than curiosity in my voice.

"What do you care? You like it, don't you?" Doug laughed, and shrugged his shoulders.

"I'm gonna have to get me one of them to hang from the rearview mirror," Doug's brother Pierce said, reaching for it.

"You don't have a car," I reminded him, taking it back and setting it on the case again.

"Oh yeah, guess I'll have to hang it from something else. Wanna help?" They laughed.

"Are you going to let your punk brother talk to your wife that way? On your anniversary? Aren't you going to do anything?"

"Only if you try to help him hang his opener," Doug said, and they laughed again, though the look I passed him should have suggested it was time for this to end.

"Happy anniversary," Pierce said, and drifted back to Royal's car, where he and his sister Gracie had been sitting since we'd walked up the dike's wall a half-hour before. Our families have been close for a long time, and the near twenty years' difference between Royal and Martha's youngest two meant nothing on the reservation.

"Roy, you were around when the state forced everyone to sell their land so they could build the dike, weren't you?" Doug asked.

"Sure, just a little kid, but I remember. Man, it was fierce, losing almost a third of the reservation to this thing made folks awfully crabby. You know, we're all supposed to be looking after the world for the next seven generations, but it looks like we dropped the ball for more generations than that. It's not like we're ever getting this land back. What a mess that was. All the cops out here hassling people, people hassling them back, but the saddest part was when we watched them yank our house out of its foundation like a stump gone bad with termites. Used to be right over there." Royal shook his head and looked out across the water, pretending he could distinguish the submerged land. He didn't really remember it that vividly, couldn't, but he'd heard it for so long, he'd somehow reconstructed the events in his own memory from the spare parts others had given him. He prided himself on living through an important part of our collective history that I hadn't, again, holding experience hostage.

"You know, we had other land but no way to pay for moving the house, and my dad was running off all the time, didn't have his shit together. That was how he ended up selling it to your dad. That and what they gave us for the land they forced us to sell was enough to get us rent for a while down north end of the city but not enough to build new or set up foundation work to move our old house, so we just lost it all."

"Here we go," I said, having heard this story about a million times too many, and, as Royal built it, Harris Mounter and Barry Boans miraculously saved us all from destitution, and he omitted certain other facts that revealed these two men to be the wretched opportunist alcoholics they were and continue to be.

"Our ma chopped her braid off, going all traditional on us, mourning the loss of our home. To me, though, it's still ours, in some way. Even now, whenever we spend time at your ma's house, knowing I was born in the room she uses for putting up her canning, leaves me wanting to move on back in there, but you know, it's yours now."

"See?" Doug said, lifting his head. "That's why we come up here. You never forget your losses."

"Jeez, Dougie," Gracie said, "you're beginning to sound like Ma. History this and history that. If I hear one more time about how she and their ma, and all the other women, chopped off their hair to show her support and how she took care of everyone's kids so they could fight on the line. . . ." Gracie looked at me, knowing she would find an ally.

"Well, I would never cut off my braid for something as stupid as that. All that hokey Indian romanticism bullshit," I said, smoothing my braid again.

"Yeah, my dad tried real hard to get my ma not to do it, but she said it was the only way she could get on with things. He loved her hair," Royal said.

"Just like I love yours, Babe. So, I'm glad you ain't planning on cutting it, but, anyway, these are the reasons we have to come up here every year. I know you think it's stupid, but someday, when you're thinking about things you might lose, remember, your land is right over there," Doug said, pointing to that place inside the dike where we'd lost everything we had, "and you ain't never getting that back."

"But it doesn't mean anything to me. I wasn't even born then, and neither were you," I said, looking out over the water just the same.

"You weren't born when Jay Silverheels was riding the airwaves as Tonto either, but you sure as shit know all there is to say about him."

"It's my job to know all there is to know about Jay Silverheels. Knowing that my brother had his ass spanked for the first and only time in your ma's canning cupboard doesn't put food on our table," I joked, though no one joined me in laughing. I was the only one among them who had never lived on the reservation, the only one who felt the absence in abstraction alone.

"Neither does your buddy, Jay, or your other one, the home-grown Indian star, Plastic Fred Howkowski," Royal said, over-riding his usual stance of adamant silence on Fred. I suspect his motivation lay in the fact that he never got over our mother encouraging me to enroll in college and not treating him equally. He lacked the acumen, and he knew it, but, non-sense that it is, he liked to think he could have, if she would have believed in him. She never blew smoke for any of us, thought we should be judged only for what we were trying to be. Royal is a good gas pumper, and he can make change quicker than lightning, even without a cash register.

"I wouldn't have to worry so much about food on my table if you'd stay out of my fridge when you come over," I replied, standing and stretching. "You guys ready?"

"Who's riding with who?" Doug asked, then abruptly reached into his hip pocket. "Oh wait, I almost forgot. Here's the other part of your anniversary gift," he said, handing me a piece of paper. On top of the reservoir, where we always began our anniversary every year, he presented me the receipt for a down payment he had made on a trailer. "Babe, as soon as I get all the paperwork settled, we're moving back here—we're coming home." What could I say? What a wife who truly loved her husband says, that's what. I told him I couldn't wait and suggested we head to the city to finish our celebration. Sometimes I was not as articulate as I would have liked, but, then, sometimes he was not a terrific listener either. Doug Boans was a real sweetheart, but he remained rough and unrefined. The piece of paper he handed me was the first thing changing our lives that night, and the rest had to do, as many things do, with the reservation and the strange ways people learn to save themselves, but, as we entered Circle Club a little later, the receipt was displaced by an equally intriguing turn of events. T. J. Howkowski stood at the end of the bar. He'd come home.

"Shirley Mounter's daughter, right?" T.J. said.

"Annie." I held out my hand, and he shook it. Doug watched from the pool table. It wasn't that he didn't trust me, of course, but, instead, because he knew what T. J. Howkowski could mean to me, a doorway into the life I had sought out for so many years. "How long have you been back?"

"Not long. Not long at all. I just finished another season playing the big chief in the nut house, in Columbus, and was supposed to move to Rome for the same role."

"I'd heard you were acting, sounds like you're really making a go of it."

"Yeah, if I want to do the same role across the country."

"A lot of aspiring actors don't get the chance."

"True. There's not a lot of call for six foot two Indian actors and also not a lot of six foot two Indian actors to play the part of the chief, so I guess it works out. But, anyway, my grams got sick, and she's too much for my gramps to handle alone, so . . . here I am. Buy you a drink?"

"No thanks," I said, raising the nearly full beer in my hand. "Rome, how exotic. You're one dedicated grandson, particularly considering. . . ." The rest of that idea was none of my business. The internal dynamics of families are their own private mysteries, a fact I can confirm all too explicitly with my own evidence, and it was none of my business that his grandmother opted for her grandson to be raised by some strange white family in the Southwest.

"Considering that she never took care of me? Is that what you were going to say? Well, she was just honoring my daddy's wishes, and, besides, it's not quite as glamorous as it sounds. That was Rome, New York, not Italy."

"I see. Yes, that would make a difference. So, what are you doing for a living, then?"

"Looking actually. Probably wind up at Mason Rollins's smoke shop, if they'll have me. Living off of savings right now."

"Come up to the college next week. I'll introduce you to the chair of the theater department. Maybe they've got something. Even if it's only adjunct, it's still a job in your field, and, if you teach two sections, you get health insurance and don't have to deal with the reservation clinic. You know, only if you want to."

"Yeah, that sounds great. What do you do at the college?"

"Funny you should ask," I said. "I teach art history from an indigenous perspective, and, actually, I'm working on your father's career," I said, and tried to sip my beer casually.

"Nice setup," he said, laughing. "Subtle. I'll save you some trouble. I don't mind sharing what little information I have on him, but *little* is the correct modifier there. I think my gram might have some clippings, letters, stuff like that. I'm sure she'd be happy to let you borrow." Though Imogene Howkowski and my mother had remained friends, they'd drifted apart considerably after Fred died, and I hadn't felt I really had an entry to approaching her, but this opening was perfect.

"Let me give you my number, and we'll set up a time for next week," I said, trying to wrap this opportunity up. My group had quit playing pool or even talking with one another, choosing to

94

stare at the two of us with bored expressions. None took steps to join our conversation or to invite us both back to theirs. I suspected this manifestation was largely the work of my brother, though who could tell in any definitive way? "It's our anniversary, seven years. You remember Doug. Anyway, I suppose I had better head—"

"You know, I have something in my car that was my daddy's. I think you might be interested in it." I remained as neutral appearing as possible, but this could have been a major find for me, a key to my work. I gave Doug the "one minute" hand signal. He rolled his eyes and ordered another beer as I followed T.J. outside.

"I've been keeping it in the car since I got here. I didn't want my grams finding it, and she's kind of the nosey sort. So, I figured I'd leave my stuff around for a couple of weeks and be out of the house a lot, so she'd have ample opportunity to go through my things."

"Sounds like my mother," I said, and we laughed as he unlocked the truck's doors.

"Get in," he said, hopping into the driver's seat. He reached down between his legs and dug around under the seat for a minute or so. "I keep it way up inside the springs. Anyway, it's only temporary. The house should be safe in a week or so. Okay, here it is." He revealed a small object wrapped in a handkerchief and held it out to me. "Go ahead," he said, and, as I unfolded the silk, he confirmed what I held. "It's not loaded." While this may have literally been accurate, it was also, of course, the furthest thing from the truth.

Chapter 6 Answering Calls

Doug Boans 1993

"Can you believe that asshole thought I was a hooker?" my wife said, when she finally caught up to the rest of us at the apartment. She was breathing heavy, but that could have been from the walk or annoyance. I could only tell with her about half the time.

"If you would have been walking with us, they wouldn't have thought that, instead of drooling over Plastic Fred Junior," Royal said. We didn't really talk to Tommy Jack Howkowski much, but my wife couldn't resist any information on her favorite subject: Howkowski's father, Fred. He probably knew more about the man in Texas who raised him than he did his real father, but she pestered him, anyway. Finally, we got tired of waiting for her as she talked forever with Howkowski, and we let her know we were leaving several times. She kept shooing us away, like flies, with "just a minute" stalls, and we eventually let her know how tired we were of waiting. Normally, I don't care. This kind of talking is what she does, what she loves, but our anniversary should have made a difference. The rest of us finally just got up and left, and she had to chase after us. She wore sharp angular clothes, and, even as pissed as I was, I still had to stare as she gained on us, glowed with all the beauty an Indian woman walking down a street in Niagara Falls could have.

Our neighborhood was generally mixed, but a few duplexes in a row on both sides of the street were occupied by Indian

97

families, kind of a small city reservation. The women coordinated work schedules so they could watch each other's kids, and the men coordinated their work schedules so they could have a few beers together on someone's front porch before heading over to the closest Indian bar for a few rounds of darts or maybe some pool. Sometimes all of these rules switched, and the kids didn't mind, knowing it was take-out night, when their dads were tending to their meals. Annie's pride and the comfort in our surroundings wouldn't allow her to run, so she walked with presence down those sidewalks, continuing to gain but still a long way off when the unmarked car pulled up to her.

"And even if I were a hooker, like I wouldn't have noticed the enormous spotlight mounted next to his rearview mirror? Idiot cops. Man, I am so glad we're moving back to the rez." This was the first comment she'd made all evening about my gift of a new home. When I had first asked her to marry me, my friends thought I was nuts, and hers thought she was. They all thought we were too different from each other, but who can predict what brings two people together? Who even knows? Anyway, I hated all her college functions, and she always felt weird on the reservation. But I figured if she was going to be a professional Indian, giving her a place among her people was the best gift I could ever provide.

"What do you mean 'back?'" I laughed. "You never lived on the reservation. Try growing up helping to raise these two," I said, waving toward Pierce and Gracie, "then see how much you want to be going back."

"We weren't that bad," Gracie said from the couch.

"You weren't that good." Being older brother and father at the same time was not something I would recommend to anyone.

Trying to get those kids to behave and then being scolded myself for being too harsh, some days I had been ready to walk away. Maybe that was what Annie and I first had in common, the desire to leave everything behind but lacking whatever it took to do it for real.

"To the happy couple!" Royal yelled, and I shushed him, reminding him we shared the building with other folks.

"How many years, Annie?" Gracie asked. It seems like the only people who ever know the exact number of years two people have been married are those two themselves, cutting out hash marks for all the things they've done together.

"Too many. They probably wear interchangeable guds these days," Pierce said.

"Guds?" Annie asked, annoyed, liking secret language but always hating when she didn't recognize it. I thought of my gift, in part, as a way of teaching her the language of home.

"Holy! You sure didn't grow up on the reservation," Gracie said, and Pierce reached into the top of his jeans, tugged at the waistband of his undershorts, and snapped it back to his body.

"Guds," he said. "I bet that cop wanted you to give a close inspection to his guds."

"He couldn't pay me enough. I mean, you know, even if we weren't married," Annie said, making a little face. Even when she got reservation humor and snapped off a good one that cut sharp, she usually apologized somehow, canceling out the effect.

"Thanks for that clarification. Your braid's coming a little frayed, Babe," I said, leaning over, touching her hair, and holding her tight against me. Whenever we would get ready for any event, I did her braid and then just stood back. As she would rush around, laying her clothes out on the bed, doing whatever,

I loved to watch her, the braid swinging across her naked back like a snapped telephone line, communication abruptly terminated by a car meeting the wooden pole at more miles an hour than either could withstand. I would love to take her and make love to her right then and there on those days, but I knew better. Once her hair had been sprayed, she was generally off-limits, and certainly beyond touching once the makeup went on. She had always been self-conscious of the freckles and unusual coloring, and, instead of going with the exotic look she'd been given, Annie always tried to hide in layers of color, either lighter or darker, depending on mood or occasion. She had no idea the effect she always had on me, from the first time I had noticed her in that way a man finally notices a woman.

I was at a big reservation party, just shooting the shit with some friends and cousins, and she walked in, sporting her new high school look. She was the only Indian punk rock girl I'd ever seen, dressed all in black. That odd mix, dark skin and freckles, gives her whole family a funny orange cast to their complexions, and the burst of red hair made me speak before I thought. I said something stupid, trying to be clever, to get her attention. I called her a Duracell and told her she gave me a charge. It got me a date but barely. The name spread through the reservation as fast as a cigarette spark across a field on a windy day and stuck to this day, leaping from her to the rest of them. She was not too happy with me at the time, but the others didn't seem to mind too much.

"Hey! Get a room!" Royal said.

"This is our room. We only let you losers crash here so you wouldn't get a DWI," I said, but pulled back, anyway. It was enough for me to remember others were with us. I was trying to get used to the idea of living back on the reservation all over again myself, where you're almost never alone, no matter the time of day or night.

"Oh yeah," Royal said.

"And don't even think any of you are crashing in our room. We got some extra blankets in the bedroom, but you can fight over the couch yourselves. That's the price of not heading back to the reservation." I was letting them know other things, and all three heard it clearly. I was definitely not looking forward to the breaking-in phase of our move.

"Speaking of back to the rez, can you believe that Tommy Jack Howkowski's back in town—and acting, no less?" Royal decided the lesson was over for now. He didn't need lectures from me about what was and was not going to be acceptable when we moved back.

"Yeah, maybe he'll be like his old man, Mr. Plastic Fred Howkowski himself," I said.

"We ain't that lucky," Pierce added.

"You guys are just jealous 'cause he's only got half the Indian blood you do, and he's twice as good-looking. He's even got all his teeth," Annie said.

"I got all my teeth," I said, "even my wisdoms."

"Yeah, I wish you'd throw those nasty things out. Why do you keep them on the night-stand anyway?"

"They're in a box . . ."

"That is not an answer." She leaned back over and kissed me, anyway.

"Really, Babe," I said, pulling back, "what do you see in that loser?" I turned to the others. "She's even got a whole chapter about his dad in her thing she's writing, her. . . ."

"Dissertation," she filled in.

"Man, when are you ever going to get done with that shit?" Royal asked, up to his old tricks. "Seems like you been working on that for years. Back in school I used to write those papers in the hour before they were due, or sometimes I didn't even do 'em at all, and I still passed. Figure that out."

"What's to figure out? That's why you—" she said, pointing at him, "are selling tax-free cigarettes on the rez, while I, on the other hand, am on a full ride Underrepresented Minority Fellowship at the university, getting paid to read and write and think—and that is never going to happen to you, Royal. I got the brains and the looks in the family." Sometimes she seemed to forget that Royal and I did the same thing for a living. It was okay—I knew she was much smarter than me when we got married, and that was one of the main reasons I liked her in the first place. It was clear from the beginning she knew things I never would. You have to love that.

"Too bad you got shortchanged in the ego department," Royal said.

"Babe, go get what you're working on. I wanna hear what you have to say about old Plastic Fred Howkowski shooting himself in the head out in those Hollywood Hills," I said, then, pretending I was Fred, continued, "because 'they never give me any speaking parts.'" I know it was kind of mean, but she still owed me for leaving the bar with Tommy Jack Howkowski on our anniversary, even for a little while.

"I'm not writing about that," she said, frowning. "That would be so crass. I'm writing about—"

"Oh just go get it and quit pretending you need us to beg you," Royal said. He felt his hassling was a public service for friends and family, but, really, he was proud of what she was doing, too. She rushed out and came right back with a thick stack of pages. "I didn't mean the whole fucking thing. I'm crashing as soon as I'm done with this." He drained most of the bottle, letting her know she didn't have much time. Her oldest brother was supportive but not to the point of bad judgment.

"This isn't even the whole chapter. I'm just giving you the highlights. Wouldn't want to bore you, Brother."

"Then put it back in the drawer."

"Cute. Anyway. This chapter is called 'Silent Screams: The Indian Actor as Angry Landscape in the American Film Western.' " She paused and cleared her throat, just like she does for those presentations, instead of just standing in front of her family after a late night of many beers. "In order to fully and deeply explore the ramifications of—"

"Is there a colon somewhere in that title?" I asked.

"After the *Screams*."

"Usually the scream comes after my colon," Royal said.

"Do you guys want to hear this or not!" My wife had a very limited sense of humor, particularly when it came to Fred Howkowski. "All right, then. From the beginning. Again. '*Silent Screams Colon*,' " she exaggerated, " 'The Indian Actor as Angry Landscape in the American Film Western'. In order to fully and deeply explore the complex ramifications of stereotypical images of Native Americans in American film, the western genre in specific—"

"I thought you were calling us Indians in the title. So, which one is it?" Royal said.

"The western genre," she continued, ignoring him again, "in specific, several case studies must be made. One acting career upon which these stereotypes had significant impact was that of Frederick Howkowski (Tuscarora) from the Tuscarora Reservation near Niagara Falls, New York, perhaps better known by his professional name: Frederick Eagle Cry. While having screen credits for thirty-three films in just over two short years, Howkowski's voice was not heard even once on the soundtrack of any of those films. His career, tragically cut short by an untimely death—"

"Untimely?" Pierce choked, spraying his beer all over our rented floor. "Is that what they call it when you suck on your own Smith and Wesson until it goes off?" We laughed, but she went back to her less humorous side.

"Do you guys want to hear this or—" she started, but then our phone rang. Shirley was on the other end, telling us how my mother saw headlights shining into her living room from a direction they never should have, and that was where things changed yet again for all of us.

BURNING MEMORIES

Really almost nobody sees this happen, but it's one of those reservation times so outrageous that many people will later misremember the event, as if they had seen it firsthand, like the police evicting us from lands that were supposed to be ours forever. Even those who are present only see their own pieces as they unfold and become parts of the larger moment, their own and not theirs exclusively.

Billy Crews

"Stomp on it, man!" my brother shouts, and I do as I'm told. The pedal goes down, and the pistons pound as our car flies across the dried-out swampland, snapping saplings, screeching straight onto the bush line. We practically lift off, splitting through the growth and into the clearing. "Okay! Enough! Let it off!" he shouts, but, when I do, nothing changes. The pedal stays flat to the floor as we cross a dirt basketball court, where a lone ball brushes by us when we knock it. That's when I see our headlights reflected in windows directly before us.

"It's stuck. I thought you fixed this," I shout, the windows getting closer and closer. Suddenly, he's no longer in the seat next to me, and I'm thankful we decided not to put doors on this piece of junk field car until the fall. I jump from my side, and we lie at the court's edge, dust coating us as we watch our skeleton of a car fly straight over to Martha Boans's house. The car—frame, seats, engine, and gas tank—zeros in on her dining room like it was being pulled in on a fishing line.

"Why didn't you aim it somewhere else before you jumped?" my brother says, punching me, knuckles out, so hard that my shoulder's gonna carry bruises for weeks. Then we both see exactly where it's going to connect and scramble up as fast as we can. A second later the car hits.

Floyd Page

My cousin Innis and I are shooting hoops with some skins from down the road, near Martha Boans's place. Innis is related to her on his dad's side, so we have playing rights on their court. She's home tonight, sitting in the window. We wave, and Innis says we might stop over for a glass of iced tea after the game. He hadn't been to see her in a while and said it wouldn't take more than a few minutes. I'm always up for a good glass of tea, so that works for me. We're up nineteen to three when the distant field car we'd heard all evening grows abruptly louder. The car crashes through the woods, and we clear out to someone's back porch until those crazy bastards pass on by. I don't recognize the car at first, and you never want to take chances on an unknown like that. As it rolls out beyond the trees and into view, I see it's a couple of those Crews boys. They're not stopping, and suddenly they're diving out of the car as it flies toward Martha's house. I run for it, but there's nothing I can do. I'm fast, but outrunning cars isn't in my book. It hits the house and keeps going.

Martha Boans

I leave my usual chair in the window where I watch the world go on by. I have just finished sewing the front of a new blouse that I know, once I finish it and put it on, will bring Barry home for good. He won't be able to take his eyes off of me, even after all these years, once I have this on. I hold it up to myself in front of the large three-quarter-length vanity mirror on the wall in here. The fit is perfect. I have every measurement exact. The back is spread out on the dining room table. I should be able to finish it later tonight. I am not much of one for the TV after the quiz shows, but tonight I have an itch that there must be something coming for me across the airwaves, and my fingers are a little sore, so I pick up the remote control and sit on the couch with my sewing. It won't take but a couple of minutes to run through the channels, first the networks and then the Canadian stations, and by then my fingers should be rested enough to continue on my blouse. I press the power button on the remote control, and the world explodes around me.

Every window in the room blows outward, a million diamonds scattered to the wind, and I'm knocked to the floor by some force I never see coming. Heat rolls in over me. The glass from each framed photograph snaps and slides down my walls. My kids in their baby pictures, graduation pictures, wedding pictures, all stare out, suddenly free of the glass that has trapped them forever at those points in their lives. The mirror shows me a glimpse of my dining room and kitchen just before it falls from its frame and sprays me with a thousand small reflections of myself. I cover my head but peek out into the dining room, and what I had thought had to be wrong is indeed confirmed for me there.

A car rocks in the middle of the room, where my old solid cherry table normally sits. My overhead light swings back and forth over it, casting dancing shadows over the whole room. The car is naked of its skin, the sheet metal all cut away and the frame welded together. It's one of the hundreds of field cars on this reservation that wander through its secret woods. This one

is different from most others. It's on fire. The car's still running, its wheels spinning into the splinters of my old wood
floors. If those treads catch, the car might come further. I'm
relieved to see that at least there's no one inside of it. My table
is pushed and shattered up against the stairway. My cupboards
have fallen onto the engine compartment. Dishes, coffee cups,
even those cartoon character jelly glasses, lay all over the car.
I guess it has no windshield. I spring out of its way with energy
I didn't even know I had and leap toward the front porch.

A second explosion knocks me back into the living room.
Two of my propane tanks disappear in a giant burst of flame.
The third is still lodged in the hole near the back end of the car,
pointing in, like a missile, straight at me, waiting to go off.
I run back into the living room. A lifetime of memories sits
here: pictures, bowling trophies, the desk that contains all my
papers. Blue flashes surround me as wires fray and melt, sending a shower of sparks out into my direction, and then my
room goes dark, my electric gone for good. The flames light
my way, and I am left with no choice but to jump from one of
my windows and leave everything behind. I cross through the
frame in midair as another blast hits me straight on, carrying
me through.

Fiction Tunny

I'm putting some finishing beadwork flourishes on new dance
outfits when I hear the explosion. Sound doesn't carry all that
well through the reservation's dense woods, so it must be close.
I step outside and wave to Shirley Mounter, who's driving by
and pulling into Mason Rollins's place to fill her car's tank. A
small feather of smoke drifts up from mid-reservation. Even
the sight brings me back to my own house fire, the things

hopelessly lost, the charred pieces of your life that you can hold as they flake away into ash, never to return, no matter how much you might hold them close and wish. I wonder what that person has lost, how this fire will change them.

I go back inside and look through my beadwork to see what I might be able to raffle off to benefit whoever it is, if need be. I look up the Red Cross number for emergency help and then walk over to Mason Rollins's smoke shop to reserve a tentative date for a benefit dinner and raffle, or whatever, in case this fire is not tires or big trash or any other insignificant burning. I can't bring a lot of immediate help here, but what I can bring is the knowledge of loss—maybe even just a hand to hold that knows some of the third-degree burns are not visible to anyone else. It's not a big contribution to make, but it's all I've got.

Shirley Mounter

I pick up some vanilla ice cream and a six pack of Vernor's ginger ale at Mason Rollins's shop after I fill the tank. It's nice that he carries some groceries now and not just cigarettes anymore. I'm in his parking lot when Fiction Tunny calls my name and points to the eastern sky, where smoke is just beginning to rise. I nod, seeing that another fire is the new bad news on our small reservation. I can't help myself from speculating who, this time, will lose out because these chiefs won't allow city fire hydrants within the bounds of our territory. I promise myself to glance up only as I pass by and make note of whose it is. I'll probably begin work tonight on a new quilt for raffling purposes at the benefit dinner that's sure to be, maybe even teach Martha some stitches and get her to help me with one. I'm on my way to visit her, though she doesn't know I'm coming. I'm just dropping in, figuring she'll be alone, with all of our in-town kids together celebrating out somewhere. Tonight we're going to have Boston Coolers to our hearts' delight. We're not so adventurous as our children, but there's no beating a cooler on a warm, early-summer night.

Like most out here, I would tend to follow smoke, but tonight I've got ice cream growing soft in my passenger's seat. Martha and I keep each other company a lot as the years have gotten on and our men have done their vanishing acts. I quit chasing Harris long before now, and she's settled into Barry making occasional guest stints at her place, like it's a reservation Holiday Inn or maybe detox. I tend to stay away when Barry's around. It's odd enough being in the house that had been mine, on any day seeing the things Martha's put up on my walls, doors Barry's cut into walls for additional rooms, but I've grown used to it over the years, as you do, like rubbing a scar when it aches in the cold. But, anytime I see Barry in that house, I can picture him all over again, with that measuring tape and that shit-eating grin, and it's more than I can bear. I know my limits most times. Martha's come to similar conclusions as far as her husband is concerned, too. If he comes home and decides to stay a bit, she calls me up, packs a bag to come stay with me until he gets the hint, moves back to his old ways, and just wanders on out into the world again, drinking and cursing and wondering where his old life went, like the rest of us.

Bob "The Hack" Hacker

I am on my third lazy off-duty beer in the private volunteer firefighters' bar when a reservation call comes in across the radio. We run to get dressed and rush out the door, but out there it's always a waste of time, our jobs sad and ridiculous. With no city water and sewer lines, when a reservation house catches fire, you better just kiss it good-bye because, by the time we can get there with the water trucks, we're merely doing damage control, keeping the fire contained to one house. I know that reservoir is a major sticking point with them, but they're just crazy, as far as I can tell. We've begged and pleaded with the reservation leadership to let water in or even to let us set up several large water tanks around the reservation, so we can have access to them in case of fires, but they're so protective of what little say they have left in anything. They refuse and walk away every time, telling us they would rather see the entire reservation burn to the ground than allow anymore outside interference in their business. Man, they play for keeps, no matter what. Even my buddy Floyd Page, when I ask him about this hazard, all he says is that I might work with a bunch of Indians but I am obviously not one of them. We get on the truck, and I wait to see which acquaintances of mine have had their life jumbled and shuffled by a careless cigarette or a vengeful fight.

Chief Johnnyboy Martin

I'm coming home from shopping in town when I see smoke in the sky over my Nation. As I reach the Nation's edge, a big tail of darkness grows up into the air, a sight I always hate to see. Everyone out here knows everyone else, and I will certainly know the person whose fire this is. With every house not on fire along my way, my heart grows heavy, not wanting to believe what I will eventually see—the tail grows from the remains of Martha Boans's house, where a flaming car is lodged in the wall closest to the driveway.

I know it isn't true, but, anytime I see the disappearance of anything related to the reservoir's coming, I can't help but be suspicious the Tunny family has something to do with it. Bud Tunny might be a dehorned chief, but he still thinks he controls things around here, and he still has a mighty load of guilt over the land his father lost for us in the reservoir, and this displaced house is one of the last physical reminders. After he burned down the trailer of his illegitimate daughter, Fiction, because she dared to claim him, I have no doubt he would have few qualms about destroying other elements of our shared history. Even if this were his own house, though, he is so furious about the mistakes his father made in letting outside influences inside the Nation that he would still refuse to let city water lines into our bounds. This fire, however, looks like it's our community's other enemy, instead—just the stupidity and carelessness of our next generation. I pull over, walk from my car, and, like all others, watch and wait for this sad event to end.

Innis Natcha

Two of my auntie's propane tanks go up like rockets, shooting straight into the summer night when the car hits. The explosion spreads through the house, and her windows spray her lawn with countless shards. She had been in that window a minute or so before, but I can't see if she's still there. All I see are flames, getting bigger by the second. As I pass those idiot Crews boys sitting dazed on the ground, I resist the urge to throw them straight into the fire. Nearing the blaze, I can't even get close to her door, the heat is so intense. Her last tank is just waiting to go off, and there's no way I'll be able to help her with a bunch of metal stabbing into me from that likely explosion. Maybe I can see her from one of the other windows.

I clear the front of the house, where her lawn glints with all those fragments of glass. As I round the corner to the back side, I see her, lying on the ground, holding on to some strip of cloth, blood covering her. She looks up.

"Innis. My blouse back. It's on the table," she says, pointing back to the shattered window frame she'd climbed through, as I lift her to stand.

"Auntie, I can't go in there. The whole place is on fire. Come on, I have to get you away from here," I say, but she doesn't budge, leaning back toward the shattered window she must have climbed from. The bottom shards of the pane and the frame there are covered in blood. I look. Somehow she's lost her shoe and her bare foot is raised an inch or so above the grass. That's where the blood is coming from, dripping from her toes, but I can't figure out how she's gotten it all over herself.

"Please," she says, moving back there, so I just grab her and carry her away, making a broad arc through the front of her lawn, as the last tank goes up. I get her to a lawn chair, and my cousin Floyd has brought a wet towel from the other house. She won't look at us or even at the house, as it disappears quickly in large rolling balls of smoke and flame. She stares at that piece of cloth she had with her on the ground. She won't let it go for anything. We put pressure on the gash and clean her foot of the sticky blood as we wait for the water trucks to come.

Mason Rollins

Fiction comes in and shows me the growing pillar of smoke over on the eastern horizon and suggests we may have to reserve the social hall for whoever's troubles these are going to be. I tell her to work, as she always does, with her boyfriend, as he's the one who takes care of that bleeding heart crap for me. Yeah, I know that sounds harsh. And, before, I might even have followed the smoke to see what I could do, and also to be nosy, but what this means these days, since I've come into some money, is that whoever owns this fire will desperately try to find some connection to me, some reason I should give them money.

These days I have set a firm policy: one hundred dollars donation from the Smoke Rings Disaster Relief Fund for any proven calamity any reservation family experiences and use of the hall for a benefit, if they want—nothing more, nothing less. It saves me a lot of hassle.

Part Three Hiding Seams

Chapter 7 Matching Lots

Shirley Mounter 1993

Sometimes it's hard to imagine why my daughter married Martha's son or why he married her, but maybe sometimes the lack of distance between two people is what matters most to them. Dougie was in some ways so much like his mother and in other ways not. He's said for years that lemon in iced tea makes it not sweet but bitter, instead, so maybe he was learning to enjoy the taste of bitterness or at least tolerate it. Annie makes it the way I do, so I'm not sure who makes tea in their house or who drinks it. The way we liked it was a taste Martha never learned. When her house burned—the same night her son gave my daughter the proof they were moving here to the reservation—having never developed that taste, Martha began eating the only thing she had left. She began devouring herself, pound by pound.

 (((

That day, as the fire ate its way through our shared history, Martha sat in a lawn chair and refused to look up at the house, disappearing spark by spark. Somewhere along the way she'd lost a shoe, but her feet were not nearly as tough as mine. She'd bled. An ambulance came with the water trucks, in case anyone needed it, and we finally convinced her to get in and at least get herself looked over. By the hour the group of us left the fire and got to the hospital, Martha had been admitted and was up in her room, a small dark-brown exclamation point against the white sheets she lay on. This should have been an immediate-family-only situation, but no one could find any of Martha's kids. A lot of them had left town, and those who still lived here were out celebrating Annie and Dougie's anniversary. When the staff nurses finally made Imogene and Nora and me leave, an hour after regular visiting hours, I stayed to the last.

"I'll find them, Martha. I promise," I said, but by then she'd had some kind of sedative and had only a vaguely questioning look for me. "Our kids," I said, as she closed her eyes.

They weren't where I expected to find them, the Circle Club, but they had just left moments before. Elyse, the bartender, passed me the phone and dialed their number. It rang too many times for anyone to be there. She suggested a restaurant they might be at, but I had no interest in chasing them all over town, so I sat and had a draft, trying their number until I got them. A young Indian man sat alone at the other end of the bar, not hanging around with anyone else in the place, which seemed kind of strange. The Circle was one of the few Indian bars in the whole city, and everyone pretty much knew everyone else. If I had studied him hard enough or if the music had not been so loud or if he had spoken a couple words, I might have recognized that Tommy Jack Howkowski had come home. He was probably still sitting near me as they finally answered their phone.

❨ ❨ ❨

When Martha was released from the hospital, she had a few new clothes, courtesy of a Red Cross voucher for a hundred dollars to at least get her a couple blouses and pairs of slacks until the insurance kicked in. The Red Cross didn't know the reservation all that well. Out there, when your house is gone, it is really gone, and any insurance company with a business sense would have never insured the house Martha Boans had raised her kids in. I knew there wasn't any policy without her ever saying a word, so I took her in, after all we'd been through together.

The only thing she had besides her new clothes was that piece of sewing she'd been working on, but it was only the front of a blouse she'd been making. The rest of the bolt had gone the way of her family pictures, furniture, and a hundred years' worth of stuff that made up her family's history. She kept on looking at it, rubbing it, flattening it on the table. "There's no way I'm going to be able to match the dye lot on this. Oh, I had that bolt sitting around for a while, had been saving it for something special, and now that blouse I pictured in my head is lost forever," she'd say, over and over. That was almost all she did.

She said she couldn't eat, wasn't hungry at all, couldn't sleep, either. Every time she closed her eyes she saw those headlights filling up her living room and then that big explosion. She was fading before my eyes, a magician in my household.

At first I joked with her, as I tried to feed her, asking her if she was trying to lose enough weight for that half a blouse to become a whole one. She wasn't laughing too much, and I threw out a lot of eggs, toast, sandwiches, even fried potatoes. She wouldn't eat anything I put down in front of her.

Her kids came by almost every day, and, I can tell you, not a one of them was losing an appetite anywhere, but that was okay. I knew what it was like to lose a home, that very home, in fact. Her hair started falling out, and her dentures stopped fitting because even her gums were losing weight. At that point I finally tried a little magic of my own. I had learned some tricks in my time.

《 《 《

When Tommy Jack came back for Fred's funeral, all those years before, I knew that was going to be the last time I would see him. He called the day before to tell me, and I offered to pick him up at the train station, but he said he had rented a car, and, when I offered to take him to the car rental place, he said he had made arrangements for that, too. He just said, "I'll see you," and then he hung up.

We didn't speak at the service or at the grave, where we watched the box of dust that was supposedly Fred lowered into the hole, or at the fellowship lunch afterward, but I knew he would show up at my place later, and I sat at my kitchen table, watching the sun work its way across my living room floor, warming the rug for us. It was near dark by the time he arrived in that rented pickup. We tried to get the kids sleepy by taking them down to the drive-in movie place near my apartment, the Star-Lite—where we'd always go to see Fred's movies, if they came in the summer—feeding them popcorn and hot choco-late from the thermos, listening to the voices shouting out their lives from the dinky speakers and waiting for little eyelids to droop. Even the youngest, Annie, who was almost two years old by then, refused to sleep at first. I imagine she was dis-tracted by the older kids and maybe sensing there were more people with us than usual.

When we got the kids back to my place and tucked in, we said our final good-byes, proper, all night long. I touched every part of his body I could, absorbing the feel of his legs, the curve of his belly, the way his belly button left just a soft indentation in the center, the thick veins of his arms, the stubble on his Adam's apple, and the softness of the beard above it, other things, but mostly I traced the beautiful, perfect curves of his ears. Oh, how he loved to have them touched. No matter what he was doing, touching those ears would bring him to just stop solid in pleasure.

In the morning, while Tommy Jack packed up the clothes he and that little namesake of his had brought, I could hardly bear to see him go. I had even let him stay past sunrise. What did it matter at that point? I could already see his absence everywhere. The dish he left with streaks of egg yolk and toast crumbs, the coffee cup where his lip prints remained, the paper towel he had wiped his mustache with—these were all that would be left in an hour, when he walked out my door one last time.

"Wait," I said, as he was about in the hallway. "I want you to take this. Something to remember me by."

"I have more than that to remember you by," he said, smiling and stepping back in the door. He touched the blanket I held out before him. It was an old Pendleton I had won in a house fire benefit raffle years before. It was also the blanket we made love on and slept under every time we had been together. When he would leave, I would curl up with it on the couch for days, until his scent had faded into nothingness. "Darlin', how'm I gonna carry it? My bag's full. I didn't bring too big a one, knowing we wouldn't be here long. I'd like to, but, well, you know, how'm I gonna explain a blanket in my bag, out of the blue, when I get home?"

"Is your car at the train station back home?"

"Yes, I suppose I could leave it in the cab then get it to my rig, but, still, my bag is for sure full."

"Take something out, leave it here."

"What can I leave behind?" He laid the suitcase open on the couch and pulled out the pair of jeans and T-shirt he'd worn the night before. The blanket almost fit. I took a pair of his boxer shorts and set them next to the jeans, and he smiled. "You want socks to go with that outfit?" he laughed, tossing a pair of clean socks with the small pile of clothes. "Didn't think you'd want those dirty ones. There, that did it," he said, tucking the blanket into the case and snapping the locks closed. "Now you can make a scarecrow of me or one of those dummies they burn."

"I would never have cause."

"You don't know that for sure. It doesn't seem very likely I'll be back this way, Shirley-Bo. I'm gone for good this time."

"I know that. I knew it when you stepped through the door last night."

"How?"

"Your eyes were already trying to memorize things. They were already saying good-bye."

"I never was much good at saying it."

"It's all right, neither was I. Still ain't." The kids were watching the cartoons on TV, but we knew they were listening to us instead of Batman. We said our last "I love you" before they'd gotten up. "You take good care of yourself. You have my number."

"Yes," he said. That was the last word I heard him say. A yes, a confirmation of all that we'd had but also a confirmation that I wouldn't be taking care of him anymore, that he would have to do it alone or with the help of someone else. He wasn't wearing a gold band when he showed up, but he hadn't been able to make that tan line on his left ring finger disappear quite so easily as the ring itself.

I watched them leave in that rental truck, counted out the number of telephone poles they passed until they disappeared beyond my sight, and went back into the building and up to my apartment.

The clothing sat on the table, but I didn't know what to do with it. I didn't want it mixed in with Harris's clothes, on the off chance the old man might come back to claim them at some point when I wasn't home. I wouldn't want to lose one of my only connections with Tommy Jack McMorsey to the random ways of my husband. It wasn't as if I could wear them, either—I would look ridiculous in Tommy Jack's clothes—so that was the first time I consciously destroyed something to preserve it. Though there was not enough in my possession to even attempt a quilt at that point, his set of clothes would make nice pillow covers, and, after I cut and rearranged and sewed them into their new life, I kept Tommy Jack's reincarnated clothing on my bed, where I could rest my head up against them and dream thoughts of him all night long. The patterns I chose were complicated for such a small piece of work, but that was the way of things in our lives. His jeans now overlapped his boxer shorts in small, folded blue diamonds surrounding white centers, across the broad expanses of his T-shirt, where, depending on the light, it almost still looked like his hard back rested beneath or his soft, round belly. His scent eventually faded, as I knew it would, and the awareness of his ever-decreasing presence—that was the way I said good-bye. Gradually, nightly, I held on and dreamed that more lingered than truly had, until one morning I awoke to realize not a trace of him remained in the air between the fibers of that fabric.

Seeing what I could do, I got bold. My scissors worked some love magic for me that first time, but it could perform some other healing for me too, eventually. After the leap from modifying clothes to inventing those pillows, my dreaming mind knew no bounds. My hands and mind remembered everything about the way Tommy Jack's clothing reconstructed itself before my eyes that day, and, ever since, I had become a whiz at transforming one useless thing into something that would live on.

At first my sewing was just a way to get a little more mileage out of the clothes I picked up. Before Tommy Jack my kids were young, and money was not steady at all, and sometimes, when I would think it was going to come at more or less regular intervals, Harris and Barry would up and disappear on payday, just not show up when it came time for them to arrive home. I would wait for a while and then feed the kids when they got too cranky from waiting. Eventually, I would eat, too, and go to bed or eat, or, if I was strong enough, get Fred Howkowski to watch the kids, grab Martha, and we would try to hunt them down, before they crossed the border into Canada.

Once they would get up there with their old connections, at the reservation in Maniwakee they came from, nine hours away, who knows when we would see them again. It was a good thing for them they were such talented ironworkers. They were always hired back whenever they decided to show up again. Good for them but not so good for us. This advantage meant their disappearances and reappearances became a regular part of our lives, like they were some magicians in the enchanted box getting sawed in half, and we would wait and wonder what door they might reappear in and when it might occur, parading around as if they'd never been gone, legs miraculously reattached.

While Martha and I had known each other before those two married us, we really stitched our friendship together in the years of continually waiting for our men to return. Barry might even still be around now, but, after Harris died, his friend spent more and more time away from his wife and went back to his family in Canada, instead. Maybe she's still waiting. I couldn't say. We don't talk about those things anymore. There are times in our lives where the stains and tears are permanent, and we salvage what we can and try to move on, pretending this was the way we meant for things to happen.

Martha stayed with me when Harris demanded I get a blood test from Tommy Jack, and I told him that I didn't have to. I took out the dog tags Tommy Jack had given me—I'd kept them hidden away all that time—and I showed him that he and Tommy Jack and Annie all had the same blood type, but the fact that I had the tags at all was proof enough for Harris. That was the last time he left. I had waited for a while, a couple years even, but he just moved on.

My first real quilt came as an extension of the things I had taught myself to do with Tommy Jack's clothes. It came when I realized that, like Tommy Jack, Harris wasn't coming back, that his leaving me with a near empty fridge and all those little kids of ours had finally become a permanent state. He seemed to think all the time, even before Annie, that, since our kids looked more like me than they did him, they weren't so much his responsibility as mine alone. I took what clothes he'd left in our closets and dressers, and I was going to toss them right out into the lawn at our apartment complex, but then, I figured, somehow I would get charged for their disposal. Instead, I just made sure he couldn't wear them anymore if he ever came calling for them, and I started hacking away with scissors, and not only the seams, mind you, but anywhere, randomly, so, even if he thought he was going to find some woman he'd been shacked up with to sew on them for him, there wouldn't be much left for her to work with.

My scissors worked their magic on his clothes but also on me that day. The fragments falling randomly to my floor began to take on new shapes, relate to one another in different ways from how they had with Tommy Jack's. There was the time Harris took us all on a picnic down at Fort Niagara, shortly after Fred had been drafted, and told stories long into the night, wrapping our little boy Danforth in his big flannel shirt in front of the fire. There were the jeans he would make Royal try on once a month, to measure his growth into a man, sometimes cinching the ass end, so Royal would think he was growing up as fast as he wanted. There were the boxers he would wear to bed, the ones with the fly button closed, that he would push at from the inside as I unbuttoned them, making me laugh. Though Harris might have forgotten these times in his curmudgeonly ways, I never did. He was the one who always left.

I'd never been what you would call the creative kind, but there in those strips and scraps were the accumulated moments we had been a household. A perfect image of what a quilt might look like emerged fully, formed in my head. These randomly cut pieces of flannel and denim, work pants and cotton T-shirts, held us together, shifting before my bare feet on the floor of our cheap apartment. Since I didn't really know all that much about what I was doing—had only done the one before—I started small, and each one of our kids got a quilt from their father's clothes.

Harris never asked a single question, and, though it would have been wonderful if he had silently noticed the quilts, I doubt he did. By then he only came for visits. Wherever he was keeping his clothes, it was no longer at my place. I saw perfectly good clothes for him at the Dig-digs, but I'd be damned if I were rewarding him for running off, even once. While at first I went after what clothes we no longer had anymore use for, around the apartment, the better I got, the more adventurous I got, and the more my passions grew for fabric that would wrestle my dreams into tight-woven reality. Maybe sometimes I even bought a bolt of goods, knowing I couldn't use it for anything other than my next piece, when maybe I should have been concentrating on my kids' clothes more, but we never had to worry about cold winter nights.

《 《 《

"That blouse don't have to be lost forever," I said to Martha, all this time later. I got her a bolt of the same cloth she'd come here with, knowing that she'd be right. The match would be close but not close enough to wear as a blouse. Anyone with half a good eye would notice the difference.

I kept it in my hall closet, and, the next time she pulled out that blouse front, I grabbed my scissors and sliced straight into it. Her eyes grew wide, but my scissors were sharp, and I was done splitting it before she could snatch it away. "Okay," I said to her, "now you can stop fretting over this loss and move on." She tried taking my scissors away, maybe even to stab me, she's just that way, but she'd lost enough weight that I could take her if need be. It wouldn't come to that. Most of her fight was gone by then.

I got the bolt from out of the closet and spread it across the table. "It's not the same," she said, looking at it, not even needing her strips to see this.

"It doesn't have to be," I said, cutting into it. "Go get my box of bolts from the back bedroom." There were some remnants in there that would complement this piece and hers. I threaded the eye with a good strong line, knotted it, held it to her, and invited her into the box. She picked it up and began reconstructing her life in the way only a woman who has lost nearly everything can.

Chapter 8 Tanning Hides

Shirley Mounter 2001

"That woman is driving me nuts," Annie said, walking in my door, carrying am armload of boxes. This was not an uncommon phrase for her. It had been her greeting as she entered my place, more or less, for the last seven years. My daughter seemed to always forget that Martha Boans had been my friend for more years than Annie had been in this world. She had someone else with her, someone who was not family, technically, or at least she didn't know how tied we've all been to one another for years, but that's because I never told her.

"Tea?" I asked in response, pouring three glasses of iced tea from the fresh pitcher I always have on hand. Royal can go through a pitcher in a half-hour, if I don't scold at him. I try not to do this too much, try not to take up too much space, fill the place with my presence, since I came back here to live. He asked me to move in, certainly, after he and his wife split, but who knows how much of that he really meant, and there we were, five years later, still living in the same place, playing out routines we were both comfortable with, if not entirely happy.

"Ma, you know T.J. What's this bucket and rope doing in the middle of the room?" she said by way of introduction to the young man sitting at my table with her. He had grown up as good-looking as they all claimed, tall and broad, in a real fierce, traditional way, sharp features, knocked out with a whet-stoned chisel, like his face was made of flint. He kept a shiny black braid in the way my daughter claimed to hate on her husband these days, not a hair out of place, nothing coming untucked.

"Leaky roof, and you never know when it's going to rain when you're out, so I keep it there just in case. The water comes in, trickles down the rope and into the bucket, all quiet and nice, no more dripping to give me a headache, and I still like to save it for washing my hair," I told her, and then turned to the young man. "You were just about this big," I said, handing him the tallest of the three glasses, "the last time I saw you. I think you might have even been sleeping with Annie here." A look crossed from her to him that says, if this hadn't been true recently, they'd been thinking about it, anyway. It's been no secret that, in the seven years since Tommy Jack Howkowski came back, he and my daughter have been friendly. They teach at the same place, go to the same gatherings. It was a natural. He'd been around the country, from what I hear, playing the role of the chief in nearly any revival of that play about the crazy people, the one with the cuckoo's nest. I bet if he never sees another drinking fountain in his life, he'll be a happy man, the number of fake ones he's had to rip out of stage floors and throw against a fake window that only leads you to another wall, painted like the sky.

The only thing that brought him back this way was his grandparents getting sick and needing someone to take care of them. He got that job down to the college, teaching acting, part-time first, then the real deal. By the time Imogene passed on and Gary Lou moved back in with Dick, leaving the young man alone in this world again, he had gotten comfortable, found himself a home at that college.

You know how people talk. It didn't take more than a week of having lunch together in the college cafeteria for people to talk, but Annie's never been the kind to take much stock in what others think of her, and it's served her well. I always knew she was going to be the smart one, but sometimes she liked it too much, like bringing this Tommy Jack here, she had to show off to me that, if she waited long enough, she could always get what she wanted.

The time I mentioned, she was just two years old, probably still in training pants and drinking a bubba, and the boy was four years old, getting ready to go to school for the first time, when Tommy Jack McMorsey brought him back here to attend his father's funeral. I've been able to manage not seeing him in these seven years since he's come back—quite a trick on this reservation of a thousand people, all sharing the ins and outs of their lives with each other, either willing or unwilling.

"That was a long time ago," the young man said. It was there, the one thing I'd hoped to not hear. Everyone had talked for months, when we heard he was going to be on that law TV show, playing some Oklahoma Indian trying to get his adopted kid back, no less. Mason Rollins even had a countdown calendar for the month the show was to be on, made with this young man's picture, posed all professional like, and he passed this out to anyone who came to his smoke shops, free of charge, where you could x out the days until that one. I put in a VCR tape, like most everyone out here, and recorded it, but that first night, the night he was actually coming across the airwaves and through the big trees in my front yard, I watched it with the sound on my TV turned all the way down to nothing.

The next time I watched it, I allowed the sound up a little, to follow the story, and his voice sounded okay that time. The last time I got the urge, I kept the sound up to where I naturally leave it for my stories and quiz shows and what have you.

"Your voice sounds different than it did on the TV," I said, and that was the truth. That moment the proper, sharp articulation of the west Texas twang belonging to the woman who raised him was clearly laced into even that simple comment, the vowels and consonants of her hello, answering a phone, the only word I had ever heard her speak, reshaped, revealing themselves. It was the other voice, though, that embedded itself in my heart, the way a piece of broken glass on a kitchen floor does to your feet, working itself in deeper, the more you twitch to pull it out, ignoring all the blood leaking out around the edges, before your soles grew leathery tough, like a dog's feet, to the point where you can cross snow barefoot, and only then, maybe, they'll bleed again for you.

"Yes," he dragged, and I heard it clearly there, "they looped my voice." I pictured his voice, the part of it that sounded like McMorsey, tied like a bronco from those stupid rodeo shows he always wanted to watch Saturday afternoons on the "Wide World of Sports," waiting to bust loose some more.

"Looped."

"Yes, Ma'am," he dragged again, "they show the piece of the film or video, whatever, over and over again, while an actor practices the line, to match up with the exact timing of the way it was spoken in the shot, and then they rerecord it. It's a pretty common practice, mostly having to be done to get rid of environmental noise, things they had no control over in the shot. It's particularly a problem on location shoots. Sirens, horns honking, planes going by, even the wind or the dolly track—the mics pick up on all of that, and then the whole scene has to be looped."

"So, what do they show it on, like a VCR?" He had the confidence of Tommy Jack, telling things as if he'd done them for years on end, but I knew as well as he did that it was the first time he'd ever been looping.

"I don't really even know. That was what I meant to explain. They needed the character I was playing to be from Oklahoma, and, likely, no one would have given a rat's ass, excuse me, given a care in the world, but someone high up was from Oklahoma originally, and they said my accent was clear out of the flats of Texas and nowhere else, and particularly not near their fine state, so they had someone else loop my lines. Technically, I was credited with a speaking part, but, as of right now, my voice has not yet made it out over the air."

I could have shut my eyes and listened to his voice forever. That was why I didn't want to hear it in the first place and almost taught myself to read lips, just so I could follow that show and not get addicted to that voice all over again. He sounded so much like the man who raised him but a softer version, a version who had not seen the things Tommy Jack McMorsey and Fred Howkowski had seen over there in the war, a voice that had not been tanned.

These kids, and they're certainly no kids anymore, they don't even hear the tan in our voices. They think you haven't lived unless you've lived in their time, with them. They don't remember the war, the way they used to ask about the "pea stalks" that were always on the TV when they were growing up or why I would fly into the room, and any other adult who happened to be around would, too, when they interrupted the kids' TV programs with the progress of the talks. They think we've been old forever, like being sixty-five stopped me from knowing anything, like my own ma didn't get on my nerves, the way I get on theirs. In their eyes you've always been whatever age you are now. They don't like to remember when you were young enough to cry about men, to feel that voice drawing into you like glass into a bare foot, going so deep even a basswood poultice would have a hard time pulling it out. Back then, you were so young that your skin was not so tough.

That's what old is, the end result of the gradual process of tanning your own hide, and, while the last step is taking all the scraps and stitching them back together into some recognizable form and throwing out the parts that aren't too useful—too small or too weak—step one is gutting yourself. You stick that knife into your soft belly, drive deep and pull straight up, watching your innards fall to the floor and slide away from you as you feel yourself getting colder and further away. After you're empty, you slide the knife down to the hands and feet, and then you begin peeling everything back, knowing it's going to tear somewhere, somehow, but also knowing you're a good enough seamstress and can do the job when called to.

"You know," I said to my daughter, not inviting that voice from the young man anymore, "if you would maybe take an interest, things wouldn't be all that hard at your house. I don't know. Ask her about her quilts."

"Those goddamned quilts! That's what started this." Whenever she gets aggravated, Annie loses the encyclopedia voice she gained as a child, and the quilts are the easiest button for her. She got up from the table and poured herself some more tea and was nearly to the fridge before she remembered she had a guest here and filled his glass without asking if he wanted more. My daughter's guest seemed to like my iced tea, or, if he didn't, he at least had the manners to not say.

Annie always brought it back to me. Once she got to be a reader, she claimed her red hair, like mine and all the other kids' hair, too, was like *The Scarlet Letter*, but I had cheated on that test in high school, that book being way too big and way too boring for me to get much beyond the first few pages. So, she explained that almost all the Indians we knew were mixed bloods somewhere down the line, but our red hair just screamed "white people" as far as she was concerned. Every time she looked into a mirror, she saw the way I've made her career as a "professional Indian" just that much harder. She probably chased after this young man for that very reason. They all believed he was a quarter-white and raised white, but he looked like he just walked off the plains about a hundred years ago and into my kitchen, big as life, just like his father. His real father, not the man who raised him—Tommy Jack was white as a sheet in the winter and in the summer almost as red as his own hair, like he'd been rubbed all night with a cabbage grater.

"Ma, why couldn't you teach her how to get her own damned place to live, instead of how to make stupid quilts?" Annie could sometimes be as dumb as a post, and I do not mean on how discovering your own talent is a remarkable accomplishment in itself but in the ways she refused to see all the things around her in any light other than the one most convenient for her.

"Don't you think I might need to teach myself that, first?" I asked. After Harris finally died, bloated and nearly toothless, all those years later, Royal asked me to come and move in with him. Harris and I hadn't lived together in many years, but Royal must have thought, as long as I had my own place, the old man might just come on home sometime. He never did, though, in the thirty years since he'd said he was leaving for good.

Harris had at least had the good graces to not go and die in the streets or alone. In fact, he was here in this trailer. That may be why Royal asked me to come live with him, afterward, feeling guilty. He knew his father, like everyone else knew him, and Harris showed up here one night, shit in his pants and three abscessing teeth in his head, begging for a beer to make it stop throbbing. Royal made him a bed in the bathtub, covering him with one of my good pieces, no less, and gave him the beer on a promise that he go to the clinic dentist in the morning and get those teeth yanked. He took the old man's pants off and threw them in the garbage, and, as Harris laughed and told him he was just like his mother, Royal went back to his own bedroom and got out the last pair of jeans his ex-wife had given him, and he set them on the toilet for the old man to put on in the morning. Harris never made it out of the bathtub. A deal is a deal, though, and Royal didn't want the old man's ghost to come knocking for those jeans, so he sent them along with Harris, the next day, to get buried in.

This trailer was without a woman's touch for not such a long time, but I never made it my own. When Royal wanted his wife's presence gone, then he would do something with her stuff. Five years later the rooster clock she put up in the dining room was still there, and that newsprint American flag she got from the Sunday paper some year, all yellowing and faded, still sat tacked to the kitchen wall. I bet when he takes it down a patch of the darker original color rests on the wall behind it. I know, because I never really got rid of Harris, though I was about down to his last three or four shirts. The week Royal asked me to pack up my stuff and move here, I left a lot at the curb, but anything that had belonged to Harris I brought with me.

Though we hadn't lived together since about the time Annie was born, Harris and I still kept tabs on each other. I knew where he was living when he kept a place of his own and most times when he was wandering. I went to the laundry and picked up the work clothes he had there, after he'd died, and asked them if I could keep the tags after I turned them in. He always put my number on them, in case he had to move suddenly in the night, which happened more often than not. I didn't want to, but I had my phone shut off a few days later and made my move. That number would no longer be mine, but his signature was still on those sheets of paper. He'd handled them, brittle, stained, cracked fingernails, and all. He was a funny sort like that. He might get so drunk he'd shit in his jeans, but he still always took his shirts to the laundry to be pressed.

So, I have spent these last five years rearranging pieces of paper in a scrapbook—photos, old matchbooks, empty cigarette packs, grocery store lists, anything that would reconstruct the days he was home and close the gaps of when he would disappear—carefully building a new life for him, the way I had with Tommy Jack and a lot less material.

"Ma, I'm making great strides in my new work on Fred Howkowski, and T.J. here—"

"T.J.?" This was the second time she had called him that.

"That would be me, Ma'am. I had to come up with something back home in Texas. My daddy and I, my adopted daddy and I, could never tell who was being called, since we shared a name. He and my momma had taken to calling me 'Boy,' but that stopped working as I got older. Besides, I always felt like I was in a Johnny Weissmuller *Tarzan* movie when they called me that, so I just started using my initials, and I got to liking the sound of it, so that's my professional name now. It's even what's on my SAG card."

I didn't know what a sag card was, but I didn't want to give Annie the satisfaction of catching me there. She needed perspective. If she could have been there that night, instead of off in the city, she would have gotten perspective then, too, but some things are too much to bear, and the rest of us carried that one.

"Things happen to people," I said, turning back to my daughter, "and they need something to hang onto. You wouldn't know. You weren't there that night, now, were you? The night of the fire?" I reminded her, as she threw Martha up into my face again. Sometimes this worked, sometimes not. I suspected this was not going to be one of the more successful times.

"You know I wasn't. It was our anniversary, and we spent it the way we spent all of our anniversaries back then." She leaned against the wall in my kitchen and eyed the rope leading up to my ceiling. The rings of dark stain irritated her like they used to in our apartment all her growing-up years. In the city we just had buckets or old coffee cans or whatever was available to deal with it. I used to try to make her feel good by washing her hair in the rainwater, telling her it was better for her, and I washed my own hair that way, too. I had washed Tommy Jack's hair that way, those few occasions I was able to do that, when my hands were soft, and he enjoyed me massaging shampoo into his beard. My daughter eventually grew tired of her mother's ways and started saving money to buy all kinds of fancy hairstyles and conditioners.

"And it wasn't you who took her into your apartment, right after the fire. That was me, too," I reminded her.

"Yes, I know, but I've been stuck with her ever since. We thought the two of you were happy living together. When Doug asked her to move in with us in our new trailer, we didn't expect her to say yes," she said in her most droll and sarcastic voice, rolling those green eyes, so much like his, at me.

"Never make an invitation you don't mean," I said.

"You're a little late with that advice, by about seven years," she said. "Do you know what she did with those talents you taught her this time?" Annie asked. Of course, I didn't, but I was sure to, at some point, if not from her then from Dougie or maybe even Martha.

"Anyway," she continued, dropping the story I would eventually hear, "T.J. and I are going down to New York. He's doing an audition tape. That man who raised him was good friends with Fred Howkowski, wasn't he? You think he might have some information that would be useful for me?" She watched me, for any response, but I'd had thirty years to practice by that point. This young man wasn't the only actor in this house. He looked down at the near-empty glass of iced tea, pretending he was as thirsty as a dying man in the desert. I had thought he was more like his real father, trying to break into the movies and all, but it seemed then like he inherited more than his accent from Tommy Jack McMorsey, pretending he didn't know the answers to those questions.

"Leave the dead alone," I said. "They're not asking everyone questions about you, so why are you pestering them?"

Looks passed between them again, and I wasn't sure what they'd told one another yet or if they ever would. I still wasn't sure Annie would ever ask the bigger question of me, as close as she was getting to it. She started this pattern a while back, even as a girl, never getting her skin really tough enough to tan. As soon as she took the hide scraper across the topmost layer, she dropped it and ran off in some other direction. In this case the scraper was her mother-in-law, Martha Boans, maybe even me, too. Martha and me, we were always sharp women.

"Anyway, I'm moving in for a while, Mom. Just storing things for now. And, when we get back from New York, I'll get settled into a new place, probably an apartment in the city."

"You're welcome to stay here as long as you want."

"Ma, this isn't even your place. It's Royal's. I'm thinking about contacting Mr. McMorsey, to see if he has any insight that would be useful for my dissertation, but maybe that's for next year. T.J. here has plenty of information to keep me busy until then. Do you remember him well, Ma?"

Tommy Jack McMorsey was suddenly center stage in my life again, up to his old tricks, reappearing out of nowhere, just like my old man. Back in those years, long ago, I would wake up sometimes in the middle of the night, startled, Harris climbing on top of me, and sometimes I just found him in the morning, drinking coffee in front of the stove, like he had just slipped from our bed before I had stirred, to surprise me with a fresh pot. He was coming home less and less in those days, and one night Tommy Jack just showed up in my life. He was a very nice man but also very free. Harris wasn't coming back, and, since he'd been around with who knows who all, my keeping company with this man wouldn't do anyone any harm. He lived in Texas, anyway—it wasn't like he would give that up or like he would be back much, and by that point I had almost grown used to people and places disappearing on me. He used to joke, said if we ever had kids, he could still deny they were his, since we both had red hair, but his was lighter than mine.

"Just vague things. Nothing useful."

"Well, I have some things to take care of, and then we're leaving for New York. I'll call from the city, and we'll be back in a couple weeks or so. Maybe you'll have remembered something by then. If Doug comes here, don't tell him where I am. It's no longer his business."

Annie thought she could stop loving someone in an instant, shut off a marriage like a light switch, but these things are never so easy. She'd finally gotten the hide scraper out for a serious session, and she'd sharpened it good. She was likely to take it to all kinds of crazy lengths, but, maybe when that hide scraper really gets you, it takes you all the way with it. I tried to help pull back on it some, but, when a scraper tastes blood, it's there, on you, and hungry. This time, when she makes contact, she won't stop. She's pulling it hard across herself, over and over, until she gleams. I hope she's got a needle and thread with her, as she makes her new way in this world as a single woman, because, when you do it that way, you always need to go back and make repairs to the damage you've done.

Chapter 9 Fraying Threads

Shirley Mounter 2002

Today, like most days, I got to hear Dougie's story, told, I'm sure, with minor modification, because the way kids talk about their parents is different when their parents are somewhere else. He came claiming to work in my gardens here. As the sun grew to that lovely color of orange that near matched the hair color my daughter and I share, I asked him in for some iced tea, because, even here in the North, May can occasionally be unmercifully hot and because he'd started telling the story of my daughter's departure to my vegetables, and they don't need that kind of bad news—they're stunted enough in our clay-heavy soil. I could hear him through the screens.

So, in he went to my bathroom, grabbed a towel for the back of a dining room chair, took a page of old newspaper for a drink coaster, and only then he sat in the chair. He started talking about the weeds in my garden then something funny someone said at work and then some *Eee-awk* he'd heard, but, eventually, he said it. He said "Annie just left," which was a pretty good description of my daughter's life so far, and sometimes I think she should probably plan to have it etched, God forbid, on her tombstone, when the appropriate time comes.

He started in exactly the same place he had with my gardens and I suspected, would end in exactly the same place, as if the events were only constructed in one way and, if he could figure out the specific way things unfolded, he could find that weak spot and undo what was done or stop what was unraveling, the way you snip a line of stray thread in a piece of cloth so it doesn't cause everything else to come undone. So, he sat there, saying the iced tea was good, even though I made it with the lemon he hated.

"Bo," he said, "your tea hits that spot on a hot night like this." The rest of it he rattled on, and I closed my eyes, listening carefully to the specific way he told it. I could picture it as if I had been there with him the whole time. He forgets that I lived with my daughter for more years than he had, and I know the ways she does things. What he doesn't know is that maybe I started everything that happened in the story he insisted on telling to my squashes and snap beans by teaching his mother a particular way of surviving all the grievances that come our way. Dougie's version started when he walked into the trailer he has shared with my daughter and his mother for the last seven years.

"Annie just left," his ma said, as he walked in the door. She sat, like she always did, in her room. Martha's room was very much like the room I had in Royal's trailer, except mine was not thick with smoke and loud television voices, the way her environment surrounded her in a dense haze, as she lighted a new cigarette off the embers of the one she was finishing and then squeezed the sparks out into the ashtray beside her bed.

"You stink," she added, blowing a stream of Pall Mall smoke out into the room. The only part of this that surprised me was that Martha could smell her boy's sweat at all, as congested with smoke as her room was. But it was another day at the smoke shop for him, with no AC except in the back office, and these days Dougie was only pulling cash register. "Go use that shower and throw them clothes in the machine. I'll put them on when you're out. *Tho(t)-gwahdee-hot*, supper'll be ready before you know it."

"So, where'd she say she was going?" he asked, making a perfect swish shot into the washer and pounding down the trailer hallway, which creaked and shook under his heavy footsteps.

"Who knows, who cares," she mumbled in reply. In the seven years the three of them had lived there together, Martha and my Annie never developed much beyond simple information exchange in the things they said to one another. Through no fault of my own, I brought Annie up a city Indian, and, no matter how long she'd lived here on the reservation, Martha let her know there was a difference between them.

Dougie entered the bedroom he's shared with my daughter for all that time, and he wasn't sure at first what was wrong. He recognized the new quilt on the bed as the piece Martha has been sewing on over the past month, but that's what she did these days. Almost any given day, the likelihood of a new Martha Boans quilt appearing somewhere on the reservation is on par with the likelihood of someone wrecking a car on one of the seven roads within the borders. This is to say, any day at all. She took what I had given her and made it her own in ways I could never even dream of.

Ever since the fire took everything she owned, she spent most of her days with other random pieces of fabric, cutting, ripping, folding, and pleating them into something new. Though I taught her, she'd gotten carried away, even in my book. Any random swatch that entered her field of vision unclaimed, and sometimes swatches already spoken for, Martha snatched up and wrestled into her own idea of the swatch's destiny. There was something a little unusual about that new quilt, but Dougie couldn't quite place it, something almost familiar, but he was too distracted by the rest of the room to really say what about this quilt nagged at him so.

Across the entire bedroom all those figurines Annie littered their dresser tops—and she'd had plenty of them forever, I can tell you that with certainty—every one of them was gone. Every single bug-eyed Indian child in a blanket, every war bonnet-wearing brave with an eagle hooked to his hand, every princess crouched with a fawn, even the miniature imitation Navajo rugs she covered the dressers with, they were all gone. It was as if a miniature cavalry had come and massacred the entire community existing on the plains of Dougie's and my daughter's bedroom furniture.

The surfaces, aside from their stripped-down appearance, seemed normal, but inside things were quite different. His part of the closet was intact, but Annie's side lay wide open, only the wire hangers Martha wrapped in yarn scraps remained, hanging on the bar, and Dougie could almost swear they moved with the clothes that had been pulled from them. Her drawers as well, while neatly setting in their grooves, no longer held Annie's T-shirts, panties, those thick, puffy socks she liked to wear to bed, even in the summer. I think she got that habit from our old apartment in the city. She never could get used to the idea that other people had been walking barefoot, and Lord knows what else, on our floor before we moved in. The other kids lay on the floor all the time, and I was occasionally given to some other activities there myself, but Annie always kept herself away from the floor as much as possible. That child was never barefoot, except in the tub, since she was a baby, chewing on those toes, before deciding the world was full of germs she needed to stay away from. I don't know how she expected her feet to toughen.

"Ma!" Dougie yelled down the hall. He grabbed a clean pair of jeans from his side of the closet and stuffed his legs into them as he pounded toward the kitchen. "Ma!" he repeated, standing just a few feet from Martha. She turned from the stove, where hot grease rockets shot up from a frying pan and spattered the wall above.

"What?" she asked, turning on the exhaust fan. "Fry bread'll be ready in just a minute, guess you'll have to shower after. Go sit downwind at the table," she said, poking her fry bread with a long fork and flipping it in the hot grease.

"Ma, what happened here? Where's Annie?"

"I told you, she just left. You know those city Indians, always on the move. It's just like that one your uncle married . . ."

"Jesus! What did you say?"

"Don't you be taking the Lord's name in vain in my house. I'm still your—"

"This is not your house. This is our house. All three of us put the money in, all three. Why am I even talking to you about this? Did she say where she was going?"

"She just left, that's all. Here, sit down, eat. She'll be back, that type always comes back."

Dougie stood on the front steps, tugging on a new T-shirt, trying to get a sense of where Annie might be, lifting his nose in the air, to maybe track her that way. He says he pictured her on Fifteenth Street, where they lived in the city those years ago, in one half of a duplex. I'd lived in a neighborhood just like theirs most of my adult life, and that was the way Annie grew up, so she was surely comfortable living that life before he brought her back to the reservation. What I'm saying is: I knew the draw, and Dougie knew it, too. He pictured her near the Circle Club, the Indian bar we've gone to for ages. In his mind that was always a good place, and I could agree with that assessment. Even before all the new gadgety things, electronic

147

darts and the like, they had the best jukebox, and they kept "The Name Game" long after that song lost its popularity. That was also the place my dog paw–tough heart met the piece of glass that worked its way deep.

I imagine he pictured her in her confidence clothes, those sharp outfits she used to wear when they lived in the city. Now that she was over thirty, she wore more conservative clothing. These days she favored jumper dresses that shifted on her as she walked and made her shape nearly disappear in the folds of fabric. Only on days when she wanted to look really sharp did she break out those tailored suits I'd altered for her just after she finished graduate school. The bright-red hair she'd always been so proud of that she'd kept it in a thick braid coiling down to the small of her back, heavy and rusty, like copper cable, now hung crooked and short in a cut I swore must have been done by a hairdresser with some serious cataracts. Dougie was sure, though, that this cut was not a mistake, as she had it trimmed back this way every month. Red hair wasn't entirely unheard of in Indian communities and was a lot more common in families like ours—city Indian families where an Irishman had clearly snuck in somewhere down the line.

One time she dyed her hair black, when she was in high school. I had a hell of a time getting the stain out of my kitchen sink, had to use almost a full jug of cider vinegar to get it done. We'd surely not have gotten our security deposit back when we eventually moved if a dull swath of purple-gray streaked the porcelain.

She had saved all of the money from her job in the school library and got a permanent, saying she hated how long and straight her hair was, that it was "too Land O'Lakes Indian girl," whatever that meant. She had finally grown accustomed to being called a Duracell, but the unexpected new name she was given when she showed up in her non-Indian hairstyle soon made her reconsider her new look. She decided being named after a battery wasn't half as bad as being called Little Orphan every day and having countless fools singing off-key to her that the sun would come out tomorrow. She hacked it off as far as she could and dyed it all black until it grew back in straight.

"Babe, I hope you never cut your hair again," Dougie said, whenever someone told that story at a party.

"Then you should watch what you say to me," she usually replied.

Dougie must have said something more to her, and he never quite knew what it was. One day she had just come home without the braid and from that point on had kept it, secretly, hidden in a pool cue sheath. She hadn't asked him if he would mind or told him she was considering it. Everything was just gone. He had found the braid when they moved back here to the reservation. Wondering when his wife had taken up billiards, he unzipped the case and reveled in the gleaming shaft of her hair. He pulled it gently from the case and held it to his cheek, still smelling the faint scent of the brand of hair spray she used back then. She had sprayed it before having it cut, probably in the same way she would before they would go to some formal event.

He zipped the cue case and replaced it where he had found it deep within her closet in the duplex bedroom and let her pack and move it, never knowing he had discovered it. The first opportunity that had come his way, a conference trip to New York City with T. J. Howkowski she'd gone on nine months after they'd moved back, he searched and searched everywhere in their new trailer home, and it had taken him nearly the entire weekend to find the case. She had tucked it into a dead wall space above the kitchen cabinets, where a small panel allowed access to hidden phone wires.

He replaced the case almost immediately, checking on it every now and again when he was home alone. The case protected her braid some, but after a while it began to take on scents from the thousands of meals cooked on the stove just below it, and in this last year Dougie believed the hair spray he could still smell was over 99 percent memory and love. His opportunities remained constant, not growing nor decreasing in frequency. Annie was home less and less, sometimes spending long evenings here with me but mostly not—who could really say where she was? In direct contrast, Martha Boans left the house less and less and now was an almost constant presence, filling the trailer with her signatures, soap opera voices and cigarette smoke.

So, Dougie walked back into the kitchen, where Martha pulled a few potatoes from the dishwasher. She didn't believe that a machine could wash dishes, didn't trust them to scrub as well as she could, frequently making note that the machine had no fingernails to scrape off hardened food, showing her own toughened and cracked nails as preferential. I can't say I would follow her example if given the chance, trusting machines maybe a little more than Martha, but my boy Royal and I have a lower-end-model trailer than Dougie and Annie and Martha. So, she used the machine as a cupboard of sorts, engaging her lifelong habit of inventing alternate purposes for things. She did those kinds of things, even way back when we were in grammar school. She ran the teachers so berserk with all the things she did with the chalk erasers when no one was around that they still talked about her those years later when I had the same teachers. I won't get into these things here, but let me say I think they passed her just to get her out of their hair and to get their erasers back.

This was one of the things Annie always bitched about, not the erasers, the dishwasher, and a number of other similar things. Whenever they fought about anything, Annie insisted on dragging out her litany of life with Martha, as if Dougie somehow liked the situation himself, as if he had one day decided it would be a really great idea to insert his mother into their life together. He understood all of her complaints, and most of the same things drove him crazy as well. He never knew when he was going to find squashes and rutabagas mixed in with his shoes in their bedroom closet. Martha had discovered at some point that the closets were not nearly as insulated as the rest of the trailer and used them to keep vegetables in the colder months. The kitchen broom closet was near the furnace and the first heating duct vent, and she frequently used this as some sort of ripening room for fruit, storing firm and green fruit one day and revealing ripe and tender pieces the next, still acting the part of a magician all these years later.

Now, most of this story I got from Dougie himself, and I told it just his way, but that last part, well, I had heard it plenty of times from Miss Annie herself. I wanted her to learn some self-worth, but maybe I taught her a little too well. As she yelled up and down this trailer I live in, she seemed to forget that I was about doing the same thing, staying with Royal, and that not a one of us has a real choice in the matter. Sometimes things in this life just happen, but I have always kept my mouth shut, waiting for her eyes to open. That she left is probably my fault.

"You're eating alone, Ma, or with whoever shows up. It's almost six, whoever's coming to snag a free meal tonight should be here any minute," Dougie said to Martha, looking up to the access panel, knowing, feeling, that the braid was gone, without bothering to actually step up on a chair to confirm.

"They're my kids, too. You're not the only one," she said, still examining her potatoes, selecting those she thought would make the right amount of fryers, listening to the air, trying to get a feel for which of the rest of her children would show up for dinner that night. I know her feeling exactly, sensing any of my six kids long before they arrive. I even usually know if they're going to be hungry or just a little thirsty. I could always tell when Annie was going to come over, maybe an hour before she knew it herself, could most times even know what she was likely to be hungry for.

"Yeah, well, they don't seem to want to claim you when it's time to pay for those groceries you're feeding them every goddamned night," Dougie said. He won't ever know this feeling, since Annie decided she was too busy to have kids, and he was too gruff to raise them himself. She'd gone to some lengths he didn't even know about to keep her life not so tied down. He left the trailer before Martha could reply, and he headed back to the smoke shop. He'd forgotten to fill the Pontiac's tank before he left the shop, just wanting to get out of his sticky clothes. And, besides, Royal worked afternoons, and maybe he'd seen Annie. Anything would be a lead. Like me, Dougie couldn't sense his wife anywhere and had no direction to take.

"Hey, Roy, you seen that sister of yours around today?" Dougie asked, taking the gasoline nozzle and filling his tank himself, while Royal filled another car across the pump platform.

"Which one? I got three and two brothers, you know, and don't know where half of them are for months at a time. The only one in my family I generally know where they are is my ma, and that's 'cause I'm like you, you know, oldest one gets stuck taking care of her," Royal said. Dougie altered this part a little, like a story tailor, but I know the things Royal thinks, the same way Martha knows the thoughts floating through the smoke in their trailer. Dougie could see him smirking as he turned his head and told the other driver it came to twenty even. The driver handed him a bill and drove off, while Royal slid the twenty into the thick fold of bills he kept in that dirty carpenter's apron he wore to work every day.

"The one that's married to me." Dougie handed Royal exact change in bills for his tank, and Roy turned and looked to the western sky, nodding, his coppery braid, so much like the one his sister had for so many years, burning orange in the late-afternoon summer sun.

"Jeez, no, haven't seen her in a long time. Shit, saw her more when you guys lived uptown and I used to crash after last call at your place, 'member?"

"How could I forget? You puked all over the only new couch I have ever owned in my life."

"Hey, I tried to hide it by doing it under the cushions."

"Yeah, that was sweet. Listen, if you see her, tell her I wanna talk to her, all right?" Dougie got back into his Pontiac and was nearly to the edge of the parking lot before Royal yelled back to him.

"She's up on the dike, with Tommy Jack Howkowski and a bunch of others," Royal yelled, filling the next car's tank before even asking them if they want a fill-up. "And Dougie, she asked where I keep the bullets for my revolver, just so you know," he continued before turning to the car's driver and asking, "How much?"

Dougie pulled up next to the other cars alongside the dike's road a few minutes later. You never had to drink alone on the reservation as long as the state wasn't stepping up their dike patrols. Groups there usually shifted from the hood of one car to the next, depending on topic and interest. Relationships began, developed, blossomed, and ended, sometimes even in the course of one night, on top of the dike. In fact, it was the place where Dougie and Annie decided they were more than friends, where they made love the first time, the glow of headlights from those they had left behind that night still filling the air. He should have thought to look there right off. It was not where Annie's father and I met, but we shared some time there, enough to know the place.

As Royal had claimed, his sister sat on the hood of her Blazer, Tommy Jack Howkowski next to her, leaning up on the windshield, sharing Chinese food from take-out cartons.

"I'm not going back," she said, as Dougie walked up to them. Dougie didn't know if this was addressed to him or to Tommy Jack and some conversation they were already having, as she stared across the cornfield below while speaking. "I hate your mother. I'm going to New York with T.J. for a while," she continued, throwing the container that appeared to have held lo mein to the ground, clarifying things more than a little. "I've got almost three months before the next semester starts."

"Yeah, right. What did she do now?" Dougie asked, falling into their usual argument pattern. Tommy Jack sipped his beer and pulled another from the cold case sitting there, offering it to Dougie. Dougie, knowing this was going to be a long one, took it, and, after he tried to twist it off unsuccessfully, Tommy

Jack passed him an opener. He recognized the Lakota chief's head–shaped opener as the one he'd given Annie for their anniversary that night the house burned. "Would you excuse us," Dougie said to Tommy Jack, who grabbed another beer and jumped off, moving to a group of people at another car.

"Nothing . . . everything," Annie said, sliding off the hood and reaching in the driver's side window to pop the Blazer's back hatch. Dougie followed her around to the back, where she pulled a large box from behind the seats and lugged it over to the boulder side of the dike, leading to the water.

Dougie tried to help her with the box, noticing it was the sort of shipping box cigarette cartons came to the shop in, confirming the reason Royal had known where she was. These boxes leaving the shop generally meant it was moving day for someone on the reservation. She tugged away from him, almost falling as she reached the incline. "I want my life back. For a while I wanted our life back, but it's been so goddamned long that you just accept this as your life. You probably like the fact that she's slowly taking everything over, what we do, who we see, when we're eating, shit, what we're eating, even who we are. Well, it may be your life, but it isn't mine."

"Yeah, I just love living with her, finding gourds in my shoes at harvest time, never knowing who's gonna have eaten some leftover fry bread I was planning to take for lunch the next day to save us some money, while you head off to New York or Montreal or Chicago or wherever the hell your little erasable calendar says you are this week. You and the big shot actor over there, the Indian artist and the Indian actor, doing the big time. Ever since he got on that stupid law show, that's all anyone ever talks about. The only difference between him and his dad is he don't get shot on TV as often. Whyn't you two try on the role of Indian son and Indian daughter, then see how smooth you are."

"What would you call the last seven years, an audition?" Annie said, removing every one of her figurines and setting them up along the rocks. She eventually came to the peach-colored plastic Indians, and, grabbing one in particular, she walked over to Tommy Jack and handed it to him. "Here, your dad doesn't deserve what I'm going to do, so you should take him home." Tommy Jack nodded and set it inside his car as Annie walked back to her Blazer and took another box to the boulders, Dougie carrying on the entire time.

Dougie spotted the cue carrier behind the next shipping box Annie grabbed. "Baby, what are you doing?" he asked, picking a figurine from the Blazer and holding it. Annie took it from him and set it among the rocks.

"You better move now," she said, returning to the Blazer one last time. "And don't call me 'Baby.' It's demeaning and tacky."

"Whoo-hoo, you tell him, Baby," Floyd Page yelled from the hood of one of the other cars.

"Whyn't you come over here, and I'll give you something to collect," shouted his cousin Innis Natcha, sitting next to him.

"Assholes, why don't you make yourself useful and work on my mom's roof?" She was always worried about how my place looked, almost never bringing anyone over. Funny, the one person she welcomed through my door. "Now I remember why I quit coming here when I grew up," she said, pulling out the cue sheath and unzipping it. It was bulkier in part and clearly held something more than what Dougie knew to be inside. Then she did the most unlikely thing. She pulled a revolver from it and dropped the thick leather case to the ground. All comments ended right there, and I bet Floyd wished he was up on my roof with some tar paper and aluminum at that moment. Some people jumped back into their cars, ready to head out if things got scary. The sight of a gun wasn't truly enough to end a dike party, but it was something to be monitored.

"Yo, Annie, get your gun," Innis yelled, and everyone laughed, including Annie herself, before pulling the trigger, nearly vaporizing the first figure she'd set on the boulders, a Lakota brave holding a bald eagle in his upraised hands, one I think I might have given to her for her birthday one year—both brave and bird vanishing in a million slivers of clay or whatever they were made of that rained down onto the water's surface.

"Baby, Annie, you love these. What are you doing?" Dougie said, as she blasted one after another of the figures amid hoots and shouts from the crowd who gathered around her as soon as it was clear they were not going to be targets. Dougie said she looked ridiculous in her blunt hairstyle and her neutral classroom and board meeting clothes on top of the dike and even more ridiculous with the revolver, but he wasn't about to tell her. "And when did you learn to shoot a gun?"

"That's how little you know me, Douglas. We might have the same last name right now, but that . . . is about it. You don't even know I kept this junk around for its ironic qualities. If you even knew what these things represent, how they contribute to the perpetuation of stereotypes . . ." she said, reloading and continuing.

"You know, you can shoot these things all you want, but it ain't going to make a damn bit of difference. And what would you like, anyway? No images? What would you have to study then? Save the lecture for your students and your multicultural sensitivity seminars," Dougie said. She didn't know most of those people surrounding her and was so disconnected from their lives that she didn't even know they were making fun of her and that this was about as much interaction as she's had with any of them in the entire time they'd lived here. He didn't say it, but he didn't have to. He looked around among them, and he knew he'd be seeing most of them at some time in the next week, buying cartons of smokes from him, and some might even ask him if Annie got his gun, and they might have a laugh about it, because that was what true Indian survival was about.

"Yeah, that's it, isn't it? Just because I've decided to do something with my life instead of selling cartons of cigarettes or pumping gas, you can't take it." Annie, finished, handed the revolver over to Tommy Jack and shut the Blazer's back hatch.

"Pumping gas puts food on your mother's table, too. Don't you think Royal would like something different? But he lives out here in ways you never did and never will," Dougie said, as she got into her Blazer. This is another of those parts I get secondhand because he's chosen to tell it to me a little different.

"I'll be back in town in a while. If I've left anything, just put in it a box, and I'll pick it up when I've got a place. I hope you and your mother will be very happy together. Maybe she'll start ripping your life and your clothes up to make those stupid quilts, and then see how you like it." Annie's eyes grew glassy as she started the Blazer and waited for something to happen.

Dougie pictured the new quilt on their bed, "my bed," he corrected, telling me, and he thought he knew what this was all about. He would be wrong, but it was something for him to grab onto. The material, the oddly familiar thing about the quilt, the patterns, were cut from Annie's old clothes, the ones from their Fifteenth Street days, her old confidence clothes.

She'd never thrown them out, had kept them in some storage boxes under their bed. He had no idea why. They weren't fashionable anymore, and, though she was still in terrific shape, she was not twenty anymore, by any stretch.

"Baby, Annie," he said, touching her arm through the open window. "I'm sorry, I didn't know. She's an old woman. They do things like that sometimes. Your ma probably does the same thing with Royal's clothes sometimes. It's not like you could wear them, anyway," he said, knowing it was the wrong thing to say, even as it came out. For the record I have never done anything with Royal's clothes except patch the crotch of the occasional pair of jeans. I don't know how he wears them out just so, but he does.

My daughter pulled herself away from her husband and put the Blazer into gear. "Well, if you need to do this, go ahead. I'll still be here, your home will still be here, and, if you decide this is it and you want your half of the money we put in, I'll set up some kind of payment . . ."

"Keep it. I just need to get out of here. This is not who I saw myself becoming after all that studying, all those late nights, student loans, I need . . ."

"Well, we're still here," Dougie repeated, as she pulled out, and the case of beer slid from the Blazer's roof. Floyd salvaged it quick, which was a surprise, as he'd kind of slowed down since he took that hit in the head under the dike's water. He offered it first to Dougie, who shook his head, then he took it back to his Nova.

"She'll be back, Dougie. I'm only going to New York for an audition taping, and she said she wanted to come along. Just said she needed to get away for a bit, and this was as good a way as any other. I think she wants to talk about my real daddy, you know, that research she's still doing on his career, that supposedly lost footage of him with a speaking part from a real Indian," Tommy Jack said.

"Be the only words from your family ever spoken by a real Indian," Dougie said. "The white half your dad gave you shows through more and more every day. You should've stayed down in Texas or New Mexico or wherever it is those white folks are who raised you. Your real ma might be here, but you aren't nothing to her, and she isn't anything to you. What are you doing here, anyway?" Tommy Jack shook his head. Those things Dougie said were true enough, but nobody needed to be reminded of that kind of thing. Tommy Jack's ma did live just over on Bite Mark Road, but they never had much to do with each other, even after he came back. I heard he showed up at her place once, right on her step, when he first came home, and she looked at him through the screen door, said she thought she made it pretty clear she was done with him when she signed off on those adoption papers, and closed the door. I don't imagine he's gone there since, but maybe he's stood outside in the dark on occasion. I might do something like that, if it were me, just to be close for even a little while.

"Maybe I oughta take that to her," Tommy Jack said, reaching down to the cue sheath.

"Maybe you oughta just take your ass out of here and mind your own business," Dougie said, stepping on the sheath with one dusty work boot, shifting all of his weight.

"Well, I'll let her know you have it," Tommy Jack said, walking back to his car. I wonder if he ever did.

"Tommy Jack, how long you been fucking my wife? When did it start? That first trip to New York City, or did the two of you wait? Maybe only think about doing it that first time?

Maybe just a kiss that time and a brush against her tit? Is that the way the intellectuals do it?" Dougie asked, picking up the sheath, dusting it off and slinging it over his shoulder, leaving ghost trails on his clean white T-shirt. Now these were not kind things my son-in-law said about my daughter, but I had some of the same questions myself at this point, not about others but about this Tommy Jack, so I let Dougie say here what he really said. You wonder how I know he said these things? This is the reservation, and no words ever stay just where they were spoken first.

"I'm not, I swear," Tommy Jack said. Who can say who's lying and who's wrong here? Not me, certainly. "We're just friends, that's all. We share similar interests, move in the same circles."

"Yeah, I'm sure you do." Dougie walked away from those who continued to party, and they respectfully allowed him to grow invisible. He looked out over the grassy, overgrown side of the four-story-high containment wall and watched Tommy Jack leave. The spring burning of all the dead growth had pushed forward an explosion of wildflowers and grasses here, and the sweet scents filled his nose. He turned around and stared out across that man-made body of water, almost beautiful in its shape, its orderliness, but unnatural, weird, just the same.

He sat and removed his pocketknife. He grabbed his braid and cut through it, one stroke at a time, feeling the pull and then the release as it let go. If she could have seen this, Annie would have called him a stereotype, cutting his hair in loss like that. She would forget that she had done it first. When she came home with her trendy haircut that first time, she claimed the braid was not what a woman in her position should be wearing, and yet she had kept it all those years, like the clothes, unable to let go of their other life.

When his braid was completely off, he sat on the gravel perimeter road at the dike's top and pulled her braid from the sheath. He held it to his nose. Not one trace of her hair spray remained, replaced entirely by the scent of a thousand reservation meals, filled with the laughter from hundreds of dirty jokes told at his kitchen table by his family members. He knew that the "Annie get your gun" story would someday appear at the table as well and that his wife may or may not be there at the time. Even if she were, he also was confident that she wouldn't see the humor in it, though she'd published a little book on Indian humor in contemporary Native American art just last year.

Dougie told himself, and me, later that his eyes watered because the wind had picked up, blowing gravel dust into them, and it's still not my place to correct his story, even with the evidence he provides me here, at my own summer-sticky kitchen table. He tried unweaving the two braids and reweaving them together as one, coils of his black braid layered into her beautiful coppery lengths, but the wind strengthened, blowing strand after strand away as he worked, until all he held were a few lengths shining in the setting sun, some from each of their heads. All the while, he wondered if there would be any fry bread left for his lunch the next day and if anyone had any good jokes at his table that night, telling them even in his absence. He opened his palm and let the wind take most of the remaining threads of their lives together out across the water, toward the city.

Epilogue **Noting Entries**

Shirley Mounter 2002

"It's been almost a year," Dougie said, finishing the story this evening. "Time to give these up." He held out those last strands he'd kept all this time. "She lives ten minutes away, but it might as well be ten million miles." This was true. When Annie came back from New York, she moved off the reservation and back to Niagara Falls. She never did ask the big question about her father that I had been certain she would. Maybe it didn't matter too much. Or maybe it mattered too much. She lives about a block from her old place—still walking distance from Fifteenth Street. I hear Tommy Jack Howkowski has a place nearby there, too, but you know how people talk. What Dougie expected me to do with the remnants of her braid, I couldn't say. I imagined he would want them back at some point, though he always maintains he's not really a collector of anything. I crisscrossed them on the firm color plate pages of the Bible I won way back in the Sunday School.

The pastor always said no one could remember Scripture verses like Shirley. Even after he'd retired, when I'd see him at the grocery store or something, he would say, "Matthew 7:1," by way of a greeting, and I would deliver the right passage, though, for the life of me, at this point I have no idea what Matthew 7:1 is or if there even is a Matthew 7:1 for that matter. Anyway, once I got that Bible, I never much read it. My goal was accomplished.

I had always loved those color plates of important biblical scenes and would stare at them for hours: Jesus washing feet, Sermon on the Mount, Jesus checking out the sunbeams coming through the clouds, and, of course, the Crucifixion. So, I wrapped those few threads of my daughter's braid between Jesus with a lamb and the blood pouring out of his hands and feet up there in the air, for when Dougie was ready to have them back. I kept things of note in this Bible, since I was the only one who knew where it was. The most recent acquisition fell out when I opened it just now.

It was a clipping that had not yet made it to my scrapbook. The story had appeared in the *Big Antler Daily*, Tommy Jack McMorsey's hometown newspaper, last winter. I get their paper by mail-order subscription, several days late, but the urgency of news in west Texas isn't critical to me. Every so often, his picture's in the paper. His hair has lengthened and shortened as go the standards for men, but for the most part he looks the same every time. Some articles are about him being a food drive volunteer, and some stories are on antiques and the like, but this last one was different. It told of how he tried to save a young woman from exposure, but she ended up dying anyway. That was Tommy Jack all over, wasn't it?

Anyway, there was a place in the Bible so you could write down important dates, and I had birthdays, marriages, and deaths and whatever, even had the official day of Fred Howkowski's death in there, though no one knew what day that really happened on. I neatly cataloged this entry: Annie's hair, May 21, 2002. Just in case someone ever needed to know.

May 9, 2001–September 6, 2003
Niagara Falls, New York

In the Native Storiers series:

Mending Skins
by Eric Gansworth

Designs of the Night Sky
by Diane Glancy

Hiroshima Bugi: Atomu 57
by Gerald Vizenor